My ideal Mom.

by
Patrick
O'Connor

Dear Reader,

"You don't own a tux shop for forty years and not know something about romance." So says Karl Delaney…and he's about to prove it for three bachelor buddies who have the fortune to rent from his shop. These three friends are about to get some *big* surprises!

Linda Randall Wisdom continues the DELANEY'S GROOMS series with *The Last Two Bachelors*. Linda knew she was destined to be a writer when her first sale occurred on her wedding anniversary. Careers in personnel, marketing and public relations have fed the imagination of this full-time writer, who has now penned over fifty novels. She currently lives in Southern California with her husband and a houseful of exotic pets.

Be sure to look out for *Cowboy in a Tux* by Mary Anne Wilson next month, as DELANEY'S GROOMS continues!

Happy reading!

Debra Matteucci
Senior Editor & Editorial Coordinator
Harlequin Books
300 East 42nd Street
New York, NY 10017

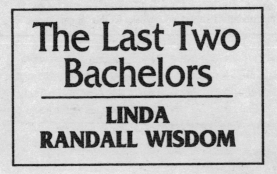

The Last Two Bachelors

LINDA RANDALL WISDOM

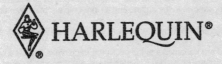

HARLEQUIN®

TORONTO • NEW YORK • LONDON
AMSTERDAM • PARIS • SYDNEY • HAMBURG
STOCKHOLM • ATHENS • TOKYO • MILAN • MADRID
PRAGUE • WARSAW • BUDAPEST • AUCKLAND

ISBN 0-373-16774-1

THE LAST TWO BACHELORS

Look us up on-line at: http://www.romance.net

Printed in U.S.A.

Prologue

"Ya know, Mr. Delaney, I'm growing so fast that by the time my dad gets married I'll need a new tuxedo. Maybe we can do something with this one so it can grow with me."

Karl Delaney's eyes twinkled with delight. "Patrick, my boy, while your idea is interesting, I am afraid that is not easy to do. After all, we do not know if you will be growing upward or outward first, do we?" The roots of his Russian childhood flavored his voice.

The small boy considered the older man's words with careful deliberation.

Jack O'Connor glanced down at his son who studied him with a look that only a five-year-old could give.

"I wouldn't worry about it, slugger," he assured his son. "When the time comes, I'll make sure you're properly outfitted."

Patrick heaved a big sigh. "Which means you'll never get married." He started to sit down on the carpet, but Karl stopped him just in time.

"My boy, when you wear formal clothing you must first learn to stand correctly before you can sit," he advised.

He rolled his eyes. "I already know how to stand! I've been doing it since I was a baby!"

Karl smiled. "Of course you do, but you know how to stand as a little boy. Now that you are part of the Spencer/Montgomery wedding party, I will teach you how to stand as a young man."

Patrick's face lit up at being called a young man. He immediately straightened up and threw back his shoulders. With his dark hair and eyes and a young face already showing signs he would grow up to be as handsome as his father, Patrick was a little girl's dream come true.

Even if he was at the age where little boys were convinced little girls were "icky."

Patrick might have thought little girls were icky, but he didn't think women were. In fact, he was always looking at women. He was convinced many of them were beautiful and kind. He intended to find just the right woman for his dad.

Patrick decided it was time for his dad to take a wife, which meant Patrick would have a mom. He wanted someone to bake cookies for him, a mom who would tuck him into bed and read him bedtime stories. Not that their housekeeper didn't bake really good cookies and his dad tucked him into bed and read him stories. But it wasn't the same.

Patrick thought it was great until he'd spent the night at his friend Gary's house and his mom had let them help her bake chocolate chip cookies. That night she'd tucked them into bed and read two stories to them. She'd smelled so good when she'd kissed them both good-night. That was the night he'd vowed that if his dad couldn't find the right kind of mom for him, he'd just have to do it himself.

He was positive he could find someone for his dad at this wedding.

JACK EYED HIS REFLECTION in the three-way mirror as Karl repinned a cuff until it satisfied his precise eye.

"Dylan should be here for his share of the torture," he muttered. He knew it was his imagination, but he felt as if a thousand straight pins were sticking into him.

"Dylan has already had his final fitting," Karl informed him. "If you want me to finish without having to start over, I suggest you stand still. I can see where your son got his restive nature."

Jack grimaced. "Suit fittings have never been one of my favorite pastimes," he confessed. He stared at the mirror so he could keep an eye on his son. Patrick was prone to get into mischief.

FEELING BORED with clothes fittings, Patrick wandered around the room. He stopped to run his fingers across the highly polished surface of a table. He faced a mirror and crossed his eyes and puffed up his cheeks. He caught his father frowning at him and quickly turned away. Much to his delight he found a cut-glass bowl filled with chocolate mints. He glanced around and discovered Karl watching him. The older man winked at him and nodded. Patrick took two so he'd have one for later.

He then walked over to the plate-glass window that faced the shopping plaza. He braced one knee on the display shelf and looked out the window, craning his neck to see who was walking along the second level. Few shoppers were out that hot afternoon, so his attention was easily captured by the activities in the shop across the plaza. He pressed his hands and face against the glass so he could get a better look.

"Patrick." Jack sent a warning to his son. "You know better than that."

He turned around and giggled. "Daddy, there's a lady in that other shop who's got a bag over her face."

Jack walked over to see what he was talking about. Inside the bridal salon across the way, he could see a woman wearing a beautiful wedding gown, but her face was obscured by a paper bag in front of her face. If he wasn't mistaken, he'd swear she was blowing into it.

"If she's experiencing premarital jitters just by try-ing on the gown," he chuckled, "she'd be better off canceling the wedding before it's too late."

From what he could see, the lady's figure was more than nice. Too bad he couldn't see her face.

Patrick ran for the heavy glass door and started to pull it open. "I'll go tell her she needs to meet you, Dad," he said.

"Stay right there, mister!" Jack's warning expres-sion was enough to stop the boy in his tracks. "You are not going anywhere. The lady will be just fine. What you're going to do right now is go back into the dressing room and change out of the tuxedo before something happens to it."

Karl chuckled. "Come on, my boy, back to your jeans again." He steered Patrick to the rear of the shop.

Patrick shuffled his feet in the direction of the rear of the shop. When he caught the look in his father's eye indicating no more nonsense, he quickened his step.

"HOW ARE YOU FEELING NOW?" Crystal asked Sandi.

Sandi cautiously lowered the paper bag from her face. There was hope after all. The light-headed sensation was gone and she didn't feel as if she was about to pass out at any moment. She started to sit down, then caught the pained expression on the other woman's face. Obviously she wasn't supposed to crumple the fabric. She forced herself to remain upright even though her knees were still threatening to give out on her.

"It's understandable, Steffi. Nothing more than bridal nerves," the consultant assured her as she offered her a glass of water. "All brides have them. When I went for my final fitting, I broke out into hives."

Sandi's only reaction was the intense desire to tear the gown off before it melted into her skin and became a permanent part of her. She would have given in to her desire, except for one thing. The gown wasn't hers and if she did that, her twin sister would kill her for ruining her wedding gown.

But that was because Steffi was marrying Greg, who was wonderful and the perfect man, while Sandi's last boyfriend had turned into the kind of slime that she mentally relegated to the garbage disposal.

Which was why she'd left Seattle to return to Montgomery Beach and basically, start over.

As she regained her senses, she silently vowed that if her sister ever again asked her to go in her place for a gown fitting, adorable, wonderful Greg would end up a widower before he had the chance to be a groom!

PATRICK CAREFULLY HUNG the pants and jacket on the hanger as Karl had shown him. His tiny brow furrowed when he noticed the crackle of paper in one pocket. He pulled the folded paper out and opened it.

He prided himself on being able to read words if they weren't too long. These weren't too long, and he already knew most of them. His lips moved as he carefully sounded out each printed word.

"Wow!" he whispered, breaking into a broad grin as the sentence took on a special meaning that meant the world to him.

The words said: *You have just seen your mother.*

Chapter One

The Spencer/Montgomery wedding

"I guess this means the wedding is canceled." Jack thrust his hands into his pants pockets as he leaned against the wall.

Candice rolled her eyes. "You'd think they would have sat down and made this decision before it came down to the last minute. As it is, it's a toss-up as to who left whom at the altar, so to speak." She glanced at the pointedly closed door.

He shrugged. "Better they decide now than find out after the ceremony how they really feel. That could cause more than a few problems."

Candice's coral glossed lips pursed in a frown. "How true," she murmured, looking away.

Jack stared hard and long at Dylan's sister. Why did he feel as if she wasn't talking about her brother?

His lips twitched in a wry smile. Wouldn't it be a kick in the pants if Candice was pregnant, too? He leaned to the side and rapped his knuckles against the door.

"Hey you two, how about joining us for the party?"

he called out. "I'm not wearing this monkey suit for my health, you know."

Dylan's reply was less than complimentary. Jack just laughed and walked away. He figured he could get revenge by sending Dylan's mother in to retrieve her son and prospective daughter-in-law.

This wasn't the wedding Jack had expected. He wondered how many other secrets were rolling around. Wasn't it enough that it had turned out that Dylan had kept a few secrets of his own?

Who could have known that the groom was really in love with another woman? A woman, who, by the way, was expecting his baby.

Jack shook his head at the memory of the wild turn of events just within the last hour.

Cori had not only called off the wedding, but she also had a few cop buddies pick up Whitney and bring her to Dylan. She'd had the couple handcuffed to the bed's footboard and left them alone with orders for them to work it out.

Jack had always considered Cori a lovely lady. Now he added classy to the description.

He'd known it wasn't a love match from the beginning. The pair were only marrying for their families' sake and the merger of the two family-owned corporations. Now Cori was doing the right thing by releasing Dylan to marry for love's sake.

After all the secrets and shuffles between the groom and the two brides, Jack wished them the best of luck. And secretly rejoiced that he wasn't part of it.

SANDI NEVER THOUGHT of herself as waitress material. Especially one who had to worry about taking orders and getting them to the right table and the right person.

At least at a wedding reception, she didn't have to worry about that. All she had to do was circulate through the rooms carrying trays of hors d'oeuvres and occasionally serve a glass of water or champagne to a guest. Since there was no traditional cutting of the cake by the bride and groom, Steffi cut the cake and set slices out on lavender paper plates.

Sandi picked up two plates and turned around to hand them to guests with a bright smile firmly in place. Her gaze lingered a bit too long on the laden plates. Her fingertip lingered near the bottom layer.

"Have you checked on the guests out on the patio?" Steffi asked without missing a beat as she neatly cut each slice. *"Sandi!"*

She jerked her head back, smiling sheepishly. "Pretty frosting. I bet it tastes really good."

"Do not even think about it," she warned. "Go on out to the patio."

"I bet Greg doesn't see this dictator side of your nature," she muttered, moving away from the table before she succumbed to the hunger pangs and swiped a slice of cake. A faux pas she wouldn't dare attempt as long as her sister was within eyesight. And held that very sharp knife.

Sandi soon discovered that being out on the patio had its advantages. She was outside on a lovely day, and she had a great view of the ocean. With the Mediterranean-style house behind her, she felt as if she could imagine handsome French and Italian men strolling nearby, and it was the Mediterranean Sea below instead of the Pacific Ocean.

She purposely wandered over to the tables set up near the railing, where the guests had a picture-perfect view of the water. Since the air was brisk and tangy with salt, there were few out there. She looked down to see the waves breaking neatly onto the narrow strip of sand, and the water was a sparkling blue as if even Mother Nature was accommodating the Montgomerys.

As she cleared the tables, she discovered the oceanic panorama wasn't entirely restricted to the ocean. She also had an excellent view of the best man. Better, by far, than any old ocean view.

Steffi had told her he was Jack O'Connor, a close friend of Dylan Montgomery's. From what her sister confided, he had all the right qualifications as best man: handsome, wealthy, heterosexual and he appeared to be relatively sane. She'd also seen his five-year-old son, who told everyone he was to be the ring bearer. There was no doubt in her mind he'd grow up to be a heartbreaker like his father. Sandi had watched the small boy parading around the room, all self-important in his tuxedo.

As a kindergarten teacher, she appreciated that age. She saw it as one where children seemed to truly leap into their own identities. Still, if she had her druthers, she'd settle for watching the dad. Just because Doug proved to be a member of a lower life-form didn't mean she was going to give up on the entire male population. Plus, there was never any harm in looking, was there?

JACK HAD STEPPED OUTSIDE earlier so he could enjoy one of his cigars, a vice he usually indulged himself with in the evening. After the way the day had turned out, he felt he needed one now. He stood off to the side where the smoke wouldn't bother anyone and he could enjoy a brief moment of peace and quiet.

"I see you still have your cigars, Jack."

He spun around, surprised to see the woman standing nearby. Not just surprised, but wary.

"Hello, Harriet," he said guardedly. "You look well."

She smiled. "Thank you. So do you."

"Are you here for the bride or groom?" he asked.

"Grace Montgomery and I were sorority sisters."

Jack shook his head. Grace Montgomery was the picture of wealthy elegance, while Harriet Anderson looked like a 1950's sitcom mom, complete with pearl necklace and conservative clothing.

Harriet looked around. "How is Patrick?" Her voice softened as she said the name.

"He's doing fine. Growing like a weed. He's around here somewhere."

Jack had known Harriet for seven years, and he still wasn't sure how to take the woman. As Patrick's grandmother, she was a part of his life whether he wanted her there or not. He didn't have any complaints, since Harriet clearly adored her grandson.

Sad to say, Harriet's daughter, Michelle, had no desire to see her son. If Jack hadn't found out she was pregnant in the beginning, he dreaded to think what she would have done. She'd made the last seven months of her pregnancy pure hell for him, because she hated her body looking so distorted and hated him for doing this to her. By the end of her pregnancy, he was positive it was her mind that was distorted. Yet, after a surprisingly quick and easy labor, she'd delivered a beautiful baby boy.

She hadn't hesitated in signing away her rights to him and in return had received a check that allowed her to travel through Europe in style. Jack hadn't heard from her since the day she left the hospital and handed

Patrick over to him along with all the paperwork granting him sole custody. He doubted Harriet heard from her daughter, unless she was requesting more funds.

Harriet never failed to remember Patrick at Christmas and his birthday, and Jack made sure the boy remembered her on Christmas, her birthday and Mother's Day. What bothered him recently was that the older woman was showing more interest in her grandson. Asking about his schooling and home life. He told himself that if she thought she could try to battle him for custody, she would quickly learn that he was a force to be reckoned with.

"Grace mentioned you were thinking of relocating here," she commented.

He nodded. "The business is doing well enough that I can work anywhere. I also thought it would be a good change for Patrick."

"Yes, I'm sure it will be. Montgomery Beach has always seemed like a lovely area to live in." She continued smiling, then turned as her name was called. "Are you staying at the inn?"

"Yes, we are."

"I hope we can meet for dinner one evening before I have to return to San Diego." She placed her hand on his arm.

"Patrick would enjoy it," he said truthfully, knowing his son loved his grandmother and not just for the surprises she brought him.

She patted his arm and moved away.

Jack watched her join a group of women.

"Why, when she looks like Beaver Cleaver's mom, do I feel as if she has all the instincts of a barracuda?" Jack mumbled.

BEFORE SHE SIDETRACKED herself any further and suffered her sister's wrath, Sandi busied herself clearing the rest of the tables that were set on the lush grass just beyond the terrace. The only problem was, the more she was around food, the hungrier she got. Steffi had warned her that morning to eat something before they left to set up the tables and put out the food, but she hadn't been hungry then and hadn't nibbled on so much as a cracker. She now realized what a mistake that had been.

At that moment, she was convinced she'd soon faint from hunger. She knew it had been said that tangy sea air stimulated the appetite, but right now, she didn't need that kind of help. She was already starving. The delicious smells assaulting her from the buffet tables weren't helping at all. Her acute sense of smell picked out hints of lamb, chicken with…could that be ginger? She dared not look in that direction for fear she would start drooling. Or worse, attack the table and gather up all the food she could carry.

She took a deep breath, closed off her mind—and stomach—to all the temptation around her and finished clearing tables.

"I deserve sainthood for this," she muttered.

But temptation, like a siren from the sea, still called her name. And like a shipwrecked sailor, Sandi was heeding its call. More like heeding the rumbling in the pit of her stomach.

She glanced around and noticed no one was by the serving table just now. There was no reason why she couldn't casually walk past, perhaps grab a bit of chicken and just keep on walking. If she placed it on a plate, it could just look like she was still clearing tables.

A quick shift of the body as she passed the table, a snap of the wrist and, Voilà! She had food!

Sandi tried not to rush as she headed for a quiet corner near the kitchen, where she could peacefully enjoy her booty. She settled herself on the low rock wall and picked up a piece of the spicy chicken with her fingers.

"You're not a very good waitress."

Sandi jumped a foot, dropping her chicken. She smothered a curse when she realized her accuser was a few feet shorter than she. She looked into a pair of dark eyes that didn't waver under her regard.

"I admit it wouldn't be my first choice of employment, but I needed the job and with my sister being the caterer, I was a shoe-in," she said candidly. "Can't you give me any credit for not dropping any plates?"

He cocked his head to one side as he regarded her. "You mean you don't have a job?"

"Oh, I'll have a job. A job I'm good at," she stated. "But that job doesn't start until this fall. What about you, handsome? What do you do?"

He giggled. "I'm a kid, silly. I don't do anything. My name is Patrick O'Connor."

Sandi grinned. "It's good to meet you, Patrick. I'm Sandi Galloway. I have to say, you're pretty dressed up for a kid who doesn't do anything. You got a big date later on?"

He giggled again. "I got a tuxedo because Uncle Dylan was supposed to get married, but now he's not getting married to Aunt Cori. He's going to marry Aunt Whitney instead," he explained, moving over to one side and pulling himself up to sit beside her. "Aunt Whitney's going to have Uncle Dylan's baby."

"An announcement I'm sure they didn't plan on advertising to the entire population," she murmured, returning to her purloined meal. She held out the plate in a silent offering. Patrick grinned and took a piece.

"What will you do when you stop being a waitress?" he asked.

"I'm a kindergarten teacher."

His face lit up.

"I go to kindergarten here after the summer is over." He practically bounced up and down in his excitement. "You'll be my teacher."

"You never can tell. I guess you're looking forward to going to school." She was encouraged by his enthusiasm.

Patrick's head bobbed up and down. "I was going to preschool, but it's for babies, ya know? And I'm not a baby anymore. That's why I got to get a tuxedo for the wedding, cuz I was going to be Uncle Dylan's ring bearer." His expressive features turned resigned. "'Cept Uncle Dylan and Aunt Cori said they're not getting married, so I have to wait for Uncle Dylan to marry Whitney before I can be ring bearer. 'Less Dad gets married first. But he says that's not going to happen until South America freezes over."

She stifled her grin at what must have been his father's attempt to clean up his language around his son. She offered him a napkin just as he was about to unconsciously wipe his fingers on his shirtfront. He grinned and took it from her. He wiped his mouth when she nodded in that direction.

"So why do you think your dad will get married?" Sandi asked, amused by the fountain of information Patrick was proving to be.

He frowned. "Because I want him to get married and give me a mom."

"Does he know you want a mom?" She set the now-empty plate to one side.

"Yeah. I tell him all the time." Patrick looked down at his feet, which were swinging back and forth, his heels hitting the rock wall. "He says he doesn't need a wife and Mrs. Morrison, our housekeeper, can do all the things a mom can do, but I don't think she does."

Sandi was intrigued with the twists and turns the little boy's mind took. "What do you feel she can't do, Patrick?"

He took a deep breath, as if his list would turn out to be a long one.

"She doesn't read bedtime stories very good, cuz she doesn't use different voices. She doesn't smell pretty. She can bake cookies, but she says I should eat healthy cookies, so she always puts weird stuff in them that's supposed to be good for me. How can they be good for me if they taste awful?" He made a face. "And she doesn't like to go to the beach and I love going to the beach."

"Sorry, slugger, but there's a lot of things that are good for you that don't taste good. And I hate to say this, but there's a lot of people who don't like the beach," she gently informed him. "Out here, we don't have a lot of beaches where you can go swimming."

"Yeah, that's what my dad said, but I still want someone who will go to the beach with me."

"I think you forgot that Mrs. Morrison doesn't feel she'd look as good in a bikini as the other women."

Sandi looked up to see a taller, older version of

Patrick standing in front of them. She turned to the boy. "Does he belong to you?"

Patrick giggled. "He's my dad. Dad!" He hopped off the wall and fairly skipped around his father. "This is Sandi, who's not really a waitress, which is a good thing, cuz she's not very good. She's really a kindergarten teacher. I told her she'll be my teacher, cuz I'll be going to kindergarten. Isn't that cool?"

Jack smiled at his son's use of his latest favorite word. "I hate to tell you this, son, but there's more than one kindergarten teacher in this town."

"I bet I get Sandi," he said with a confidence he could have only learned from his father. "But school doesn't start until September. Can Sandi come work for you until school starts? She could be my nanny. You said you were going to hire one for me. And Sandi isn't a very good waitress. I know she'd be a really good nanny."

Jack glanced at Sandi, whose red face and squirming body told him she hadn't put his son up to this latest stunt. He should have known better, since this was the sort of idea Patrick would come up with now that he was eagerly looking forward to starting kindergarten. The idea of having a leg up on the other kids had to be very tempting.

She stood up, proving to be only a few inches shorter than him. She may have been dressed in the uniform of the other waitresses—slim-cut black pants, a white long-sleeved shirt and black bow tie—but there was something about her that didn't go with the formal clothing. Her dark blond hair was pulled back in a french braid, the ends secured with a black velvet bow.

"Sandi Galloway," she said, holding out her hand.

"Your son caught me filching from the buffet. To keep him from snitching on me, I had to share some of the booty."

"Yes, I can see that." Jack pulled his handkerchief out of his pocket and proceeded to wipe the ginger-colored sauce off his son's face. "Patrick is easy to bribe where his stomach is concerned. Why don't you go on inside," he told his son. "We'll have to leave pretty soon."

Patrick's small face twisted up in a frown. "You're not going to yell at Sandi, are you? She didn't do anything wrong," he insisted. "I don't want her to get in trouble for anything."

Jack placed his hand against Patrick's shoulder and gave him a gentle push. "She's perfectly safe, kiddo. Go."

Seeing there was no way his father was going to let him stay, the boy walked away with dragging footsteps. But not without looking over his shoulder and sending Sandi a look she would have likened to that of a lost puppy. She turned to the older, more-fascinating version of Patrick.

"Don't tell me. He can wind your housekeeper around his little finger without even trying." She carefully wiped her fingers on a napkin. "All he has to do is look the part of the sweet little boy, and she'll do anything he wants."

"Except put chocolate chips in his oatmeal cookies," Jack replied. "He once told her what he thought raisins looked like and she was horrified."

"But not horrified enough to stop putting raisins in his cookies," she clarified.

He nodded. "You do know that age group well."

"I've been teaching them for close to five years."

Sandi picked up the empty paper plate and folded it in half. "I apologize for corrupting your son, Mr. O'Connor."

"I'm sure it was more the other way around." He smiled. "Don't worry, I won't snitch on you, either, and I won't require a bribe of ginger chicken, either."

"Good, because it's all gone." She took a deep breath and held out her hand. "It was nice meeting you, Mr. O'Connor. Consider yourself lucky to have someone as special as Patrick."

He took her hand in his and kept hold of it. "Yes, I know. So what about you, Ms. Galloway? How do you feel about taking on the nanny job?"

Her laughter rang out. "Nanny job? Sorry, but I don't come from New York, wear miniskirts or have big hair. I don't think I'd be right for the job."

His gaze was lingering as he looked her up and down. "Oh, I think you'd be right for the job."

"Sandra, may I speak to you please?"

Sandi muttered a "Busted" under her breath and turned toward the open kitchen door. Steffi stood there with a horrified, stiff expression on her face that warred with the smile frozen on her lips.

"Now," Steffi stressed.

"You might want to reconsider my offer," Jack said in a low voice before he moved away. "I'm at the Montgomery Beach Inn."

Steffi rushed outside the moment Jack was out of sight.

"What are you doing?" she shrieked, then quickly lowered her voice. "I thought you were clearing the patio tables and I find you out here flirting with the best man."

"The way I look at it, if you're going to flirt, flirt with the best," Sandi quipped.

Predictably, Steffi groaned. Before she could give in to the laughter Sandi expected she would, she straightened up and froze her twin with a glare.

"I suggest you get back into the main room."

Sandi snapped to attention and snapped off a salute. "Yes, ma'am."

As she later circulated through the room, she was unaware of Jack's gaze on her.

"Poor, Sandi. She is not the best waitress Steffi has hired. She does much better as a kindergarten teacher." Karl appeared beside him.

"That's the impression I got from Patrick," Jack said quietly. "He asked me to hire her as his nanny for this summer."

Karl chuckled. "Those two would be perfect for each other. You would have the best nanny for Patrick you could ever find." He patted Jack's shoulder before he walked over to Candice and Mrs. Montgomery. In moments, he had the two women laughing.

As Jack headed for the other side of the room, he heard a faint rustle in his pocket. He reached in and pulled out a piece of paper. The handwriting was strong and almost old-fashioned. The words hit him right between the eyes.

You have gazed upon your soul mate.

Chapter Two

"Are you going to call her today?" Patrick asked, waving his cereal spoon to and fro while he made sounds like an airplane.

Jack plucked the flying spoon out of his hand and set it on the table. "Call who?"

"*Daaad!* You hafta call Sandi." He picked up his glass of orange juice and promptly began blowing bubbles in it. He shot his father an apologetic look when Jack also appropriated the glass and set it on the table. "You have to call her and ask her to be my nanny."

"Maybe she doesn't want to work as a nanny," he pointed out.

Patrick rolled his eyes. "Sure she will. She likes kids my age," he informed his father. "And she'll be my teacher when school starts. But she could teach me now." He brightened. "Then I'd know everything when school starts."

"Then what would you have to learn when you started kindergarten?" he teased.

Jack thought back to the day before and the woman he'd met. A woman with shiny hair and hazel eyes that danced with laughter. Lips that couldn't seem to stop smiling.

She'd treated Patrick as an equal, hadn't talked down to him or made him feel like a small boy the way some adults did. No wonder Patrick had eaten up that kind of attention. The few women he'd dated in the past had treated his son in such a way that Jack had cringed for him. Naturally those women were not seen again. Jack didn't believe in seeing any woman who couldn't fully accept his son. While Jack had no plans on a permanent relationship, he did want any woman he saw on a fairly regular basis to accept Patrick and, even more important, for Patrick to accept her. Jack knew Patrick would be his only chance at fatherhood, and he didn't intend to do anything to screw it up.

As he studied his son's smiling face, he recalled one time when he'd laughingly declared he wasn't going to have his son in therapy twenty years from now or writing an unflattering tell-all book about his father.

He intended for Patrick to have a full childhood, and he wanted to enjoy that time right along with him.

"Wouldn't it be better for me to have a nanny who understands kids my age so good?" Patrick asked slyly. "Then I'd be really good when I go to kindergarten."

Jack flashed him his I-know-what-you're-doing-and-it-won't-work look.

"Patrick, I don't think you should be worrying about flunking out of kindergarten before you even start," he said dryly.

"Can't you call her and ask her again? Patrick begged. "I'll be really good if she's my nanny."

Jack was bemused by his son's insistence. "What is it about Sandi that's so special?"

Patrick looked confused for a moment as he contemplated his father's question. Suddenly, his features cleared. He reached across the table and picked up his father's cellular phone and held it out. "She's just perfect for me."

Jack wished he knew what to say, but not one word entered his mind. He should have had excellent arguments as to why a boy so young couldn't know why a woman would be perfect as his nanny when there were mundane details to plow through first. Like her qualifications and references, both personal and work. And, most important, whether or not she even wanted the job.

But then he looked into eyes so like his own. There wasn't even a hint of Michelle in Patrick's looks or personality.

Jack operated on gut instinct. Always had and, to date, it hadn't failed him.

Who was to say that Patrick didn't have this same instinct? He couldn't summarily dismiss it.

Jack took the phone from his son and set it to one side. "She's probably working today. I'll call her this evening. I promise. Besides, don't we have a date at the beach today?"

Patrick grinned. "Yeah," he said with satisfaction. He suddenly looked cautious. "And when we get back, you'll call Sandi."

"Scouts Honor."

"You were never a Boy Scout, Dad."

"Yeah, but it sounds good doesn't it?" His grin mirrored his son's.

"I DON'T CARE WHAT YOU SAY. There is nothing there."

"Yes, there is! I just know there is. Look again."

Sandi groaned loudly in frustration. "Stef, I have searched your face with the intensity of a microscope. I can't see even a hint of one coming in."

Steffi snatched the hand mirror out of her sister's hand and held it closely to her face. "A hint? It's as big as a boulder! See? Right there." She tapped the mirror.

Sandi stared at the mirror. "Dust."

Steffi spun on her with a look that threatened great bodily harm. "Very funny," she said between clenched teeth.

Sandi swallowed the sigh traveling up her throat. She noted the location and positioned her sister's face under maximum light. She squinted and carefully studied the evenly tanned skin.

"It's a freckle."

Steffi shot her a look as if to say she didn't know what she was talking about. "It is not! I feel one coming," she declared. "Do you know what that means? It means that after that one will come another and I'll have a horrible disgusting zit on my wedding day!"

"Considering your wedding isn't tomorrow, I don't think you need to worry about one showing up now. And if one does, we'll use some shimmery white eye shadow on it and tell people you were having your nose pierced, but the man doing it was cross-eyed and missed," Sandi told her.

Steffi looked ready to kill, and her sister was the closest person to focus on. "Every important day in my life has been marred by a zit. I refuse to have it happen again."

Sandi rolled her eyes. "*Your life?* What about mine?"

Steffi picked up a small bottle and tipped the contents onto a Q-Tip. "This is guaranteed to kill them before they erupt." She carefully dabbed it on the skin between her eyebrows.

Sandi rolled her eyes. "Stef! There is nothing there to kill!"

"The day before the senior prom? I knew I was getting a zit." Steffi muttered as she kept on dabbing. "I just knew it."

"Sure, you knew it. That's why *I* was the one who ended up with the zit on the tip of my nose," Sandi argued.

Steffi was undeterred. "Then there was the Christmas dance our sophomore year in college."

"*I* had *your* zit on *my* chin."

"Graduation."

"Right between the eyes." Sandi picked up the bottle and examined the label. "I've never heard of this stuff. What did it cost you?"

"Sixty dollars. *Watch out!*" Steffi caught the bottle before it dropped from Sandi's nerveless fingers.

Sandi shook her head in amazement. "You're crazy. You're taking extra multi-vitamins and vitamin C so you won't get a cold. You're slathering your face with moisturizer twice a day so it won't look too dry for the wedding. You made sure to set your wedding day far enough away from your period so you won't be cranky and bloated. Stef, haven't you ever heard the expression 'go with the flow'?"

"Not when something is this important." Steffi's fingers traveled down her throat. "The Parisian Spa is offering a cellular facial that's supposed to do wonders for the skin," she murmured.

"Steffi! We're not eighty, looking for the Fountain of Youth!" Sandi shouted. "Greg loves you, warts and all."

"Don't say warts!" She spun around and faced the mirror, examining every microinch of her face.

Sandi threw up her hands and fled the bathroom.

She loved her sister dearly, but Steffi's preoccupation with her looks before an important event drove her crazy. Sandi used to tease her that while others might have nightmares they'd be stark naked when they entered a room filled with people, Steffi dreamed she had a glaring pimple on the tip of her nose or a wart on her cheek. Or she'd be wearing the wrong color blush and lipstick that would somehow clash with her outfit. Sandi never knew how it happened, but it always seemed whatever Steffi worried about, Sandi was the one to suffer the consequences.

Twins were known for sharing things, but Sandi didn't like the idea of Steffi dreaming up disasters and Sandi reaping the fallout.

She went into her room and rummaged through the drawers. "I'm going down to the beach by the inn. Want to come?"

"And get a bad burn? I refuse to be a peeling mess at my wedding!"

"No wonder she sent me to try on her gown," Sandi muttered, pulling out a bronze ombré bikini. "She was probably afraid the zipper would get caught and scratch her back."

"I heard that!"

Sandi changed clothes at the speed of light and grabbed a towel and bottle of water on her way out.

She left the small 1930's bungalow her sister rented. As she walked down the sidewalk, she draped a scarf that matched her bikini around her hips and popped a visor on her head to shade her face. As she had told Patrick O'Connor, beaches were rare in Montgomery Beach, but there were a few where a sun worshiper could lay out on a towel and enjoy the atmosphere. Luckily there was a small stretch of beach near the Montgomery Beach Inn that was open to the public.

When she reached the sand's edge, she slipped off her sandals and carried them in one hand as she walked up the beach. She turned down an invitation to join a volleyball game and another for a Frisbee game, preferring her own company this time.

"In order to find Sandi Galloway, all anyone has to do is go to the beach."

She turned and smiled at Karl Delaney, who was walking in her direction. She giggled at the sight of his neatly pressed trousers carefully rolled up to his knees. She could see he'd set his shoes and socks near wooden stairs coming down from the street. Only in Montgomery Beach could someone feel secure enough to leave shoes near the stairs and come back to find them still there.

"Do you even own a pair of shorts, Karl?" she asked when he got closer.

He lifted an eyebrow in silent response. Could she imagine him dressing that casually?

"I can't imagine it would hurt your image," she told him, linking her arm through his as he joined her in her aimless trek. "After all, any shorts you wore would be extremely stylish. You could even start a new trend."

Karl stared at the young men involved in a volleyball game a short distance away. They were all wearing either colorful knee-length swim trunks or Speedos. He shuddered. "I enjoy looking at the ocean. I just have no desire to enter it."

"And yet you're down here now."

"I saw you walking and decided to join you," he patted her hand. "I understand you met young Patrick O'Connor yesterday."

Sandi smiled at the memory. "Yes, I did. He's quite a charmer, too. He tried to talk me into becoming his nanny."

"Jack did mention he was going to hire one for Patrick for the summer. The position would be perfect for you," he said. "Patrick needs someone like you who understands his age so well."

"I understand his age so well because most of the time I feel the same age." She adjusted her visor to better shade her face. "The only reason Patrick wants me as his nanny is so I can teach him all there is to know about kindergarten. He wants to ace all those tough exams we teachers give."

Karl chuckled. "Yes, Patrick does like to be the best in everything. A trait he inherited from his father."

Sandi pictured the older, handsome version of the little boy. It wasn't difficult to do since he hadn't been all that far from her thoughts. "What does Jack O'Connor do?"

"He's a financial consultant to men who have more money than they know what to do with. They want to make more money, so they go to him and he always succeeds," Karl said. "But now he wants to leave San Francisco and move down here."

She looked surprised. "Leave the bright lights of the big city behind?"

"For his son, yes. He wants Patrick to grow up in a small town atmosphere."

"Small town?" she laughed. "Karl, Montgomery Beach is another Carmel, with the rich and famous living here because they think they're in a small town. It's really nothing more than a smaller version of what they left. We don't have coffee shops or diners, we have cafés or bistros, shopping plazas instead of strip malls, and even the drugstore is called a pharmacy. We have a spa instead of a beauty salon, along with upscale shops and art galleries everywhere."

"Perhaps it is that way. But we tradespeople profit handsomely from these capitalists."

Sandi shot Karl a suspicious look. She was positive he was teasing her, and when she saw the twinkle in his eye, she knew she was right.

"All right, you've made your point," she admitted. "I guess it's just that people talk about moving down here as if they're truly moving to a quieter rural world, when all they're really doing is changing their address, nothing else."

"Years ago, Montgomery Beach was a sleepy little town that had people like the Montgomerys and Spencers using their homes as weekend getaways. Others move down and leave because they desire something a little more energetic. Others discover how special our town is and remain. Jack O'Connor will be one who remains," Karl stated.

Sandi looked skeptical. "Until his office calls with the deal of a lifetime. He'll be back in his fancy office with fax machines and computers humming all around him because he'll need that adrenaline rush so many men in his business crave."

She should have known just speaking the name

would bring the man to life. Karl had shortened his stride and seemed to be guiding her away from the water. Not far from them was a man and young boy building what appeared to be a coiled snake, complete with open mouth and fangs.

"Who will your great snake devour, young Patrick?" Karl called out as they made their way toward the duo.

"A big shark!" Patrick bounced up and down, holding his arms out as wide as he could. His face lit up when he saw Karl's companion. "Sandi!" He spun around to face his father. "Now you don't have to call her, Dad! You can just ask her."

Jack was so engrossed in looking at the sexy vision standing in front of him that it took a moment for his son's words to penetrate. This was the woman he was considering as his son's nanny?

Sandi Galloway dressed in slim-cut black pants, a man-tailored white shirt and black bow tie was cute and a bit sexy. Sandi Galloway dressed in a barely there bikini that blended a little too well with her tanned skin, with her hair blowing in the sea breeze, was definitely way past cute. She was downright foxy.

The hell with her looking after his son. She could tuck him into bed anytime!

Before his thoughts ran fully away with him, he clamped down on his baser instincts and forced himself to take a mental cold shower.

"I like your snake," Sandi said.

Jack immediately reined in his imagination. She couldn't have meant what he thought she meant.

"No mere sand castle for Patrick," he explained. "He wanted something big and fierce. I suggested a dragon, but he said it's not the same if the dragon can't breathe flames. I told him there was no way I'd build a fire inside a sand dragon. We compromised on a snake.''

''I asked that little girl over there if I could put her Barbie doll in the snake's mouth, but she said I was mean and cried,'' Patrick stated with a snort of disgust.

Sandi turned to see a little girl about the same age as Patrick, glaring at Patrick while protectively cradling her doll from the evil little boy who dared to threaten her baby.

''Never suggest sacrificing a little girl's doll, Patrick,'' she suggested. ''It's never a good idea. It's the same as wanting to bury your favorite dump truck under a pile of rocks.''

''Is that what you teach in kindergarten?'' he asked, dropping his tiny shovel and bucket by the snake's tail. ''How boys are supposed to treat girls?''

''Among other things.''

''Slugger, here, seems to think you can teach him all he needs to know for kindergarten,'' Jack said, dropping the trowel he was using to fashion the snake's scales. It looked as if they had sprinkled water on the scales to give them a pattern.

Sandi forced herself to stare at his face. It was safer than salivating over the navy swim briefs he wore. This man had a body that obviously didn't sit behind a desk eighteen hours a day. He was too tanned, too well toned, too…male. The morning was warm, but she swore the temperature rose a good fifty degrees. She opened her water bottle and took a long drink.

''You can be my nanny, can't you, Sandi?'' Patrick asked.

''Son, you have to ask her if she wants to be one,''

Jack said, his eyes trained on hers. "Remember, I told you she's working for her sister."

She looked back at him. "I've never been trained as a nanny. That's not the same as a teacher."

"But you are a teacher with all the credits?" Jack asked.

She nodded. "School districts tend to insist on it." She silently cursed her sarcastic tongue. Luckily Jack didn't look offended.

"You've obviously worked with kids his age on a daily basis."

Sandi nodded again. "I wanted to teach kindergarten from the beginning."

"Then what's the problem? I can offer you a more than competitive salary. I understand you can only work until September, and I can even put you on my company's health and dental plan for that time, if you'd like," Jack told her.

"I would say he has made a more than generous offer," Karl murmured to Sandi.

She still hadn't taken her eyes off Jack. "I'll decide whether it's generous after I hear the salary."

"Then shall we step into my office?" He gestured to two beach towels laid out on the sand.

"Patrick, why don't we make a smaller version of your snake?" Karl suggested.

The boy looked over his shoulder as the older man diverted his attention.

Sandi chose the towel displaying Power Rangers and dropped down onto the terry-cloth surface. Jack sat in the middle of the other towel, which resembled a thousand-dollar bill. He looked down at the green surface and grimaced.

"A Father's Day gift," he explained.

"At least he didn't choose one with a Playboy Bunny," Sandi said lightly.

Jack grinned then grew serious. "I want Patrick to have someone I know I can trust. Someone who's willing to go along with his games and who understands he comes first. Now—" he held up his hand to forestall her protests "—there's no problem about your only being able to work until September. This way, I know I'll have the summer to find someone on a permanent basis."

"And if you decide you don't want to stay in Montgomery Beach on a permanent basis, you won't have to worry about finding someone on a permanent basis," she stated.

"I fully intend to set up an office here, only driving into San Francisco when necessary," he replied. "I've had to travel to Los Angeles or Seattle, even New York, occasionally and I know that will happen again. But I have no desire to return to San Francisco to live. I've already contacted realtors about finding a house here."

"The Bolton Academy has an excellent kindergarten program," she said.

Jack shook his head. "I'd prefer he attend public school. I understand the school district here is also excellent."

"My sister is getting married in a few weeks. I'm part of the wedding party." She wasn't sure why she was making these demands. A part of her wanted to accept the job, but another part warned her it wouldn't be a good idea. "By working for her, I have the time to help her with the preparations."

"No problem. I'm sure we can work out a schedule,'' he said promptly, then named a figure that almost popped her eyes out.

Then she made the mistake of gazing into his dark, smoldering eyes. There was no doubt about it, Sandi was falling under the spell of a sexy-looking man who smelled of coconut oil and pure male. If she had any sense at all she would politely refuse his offer. No matter the money was fantastic, as was he.

He smiled. ''Don't worry, I wouldn't expect you to wear a uniform.''

Lost in the dazzle of his smile, Sandi surrendered without a whimper.

''When do you want me to start?''

Chapter Three

"I'm crazy to do this." Sandi threw her clothing into a suitcase. "Totally crazy. It had to have been the coconut oil. I'm such a sucker for the smell of coconut. It must have hypnotized me or something."

"I'd say it was more the man than his tanning oil. Besides, it's the kind of job you can do with your eyes closed." Steffi picked up each item Sandi threw in and carefully folded it, then neatly placed it to one side. "Not to mention, with what he's paying you, you won't have to worry about the rental on the house for at least a year." After Steffi and Greg married, Steffi would be moving into Greg's house a few blocks away. Sandi had offered to take over the rental on the bungalow, since it would save her having to look for a place to live before the fall semester.

"But I'm leaving you in a lurch," Sandi protested.

"Sister, dear, you've proven only too well that you were never meant to be a waitress. It saves me from having to fire you. Stick to what you know." She carefully smoothed out a T-shirt before folding it. "You left Seattle and Doug for a new life. This is your chance. And this guy is not only a lot cuter than Doug, he's definitely richer," she teased.

"He's my boss, nothing more. And it's only temporary. Besides, I'm a kindergarten teacher, not a live-in nanny," she muttered, experiencing a fluttering sensation deep in the pit of her stomach. She knew Jack had a three-bedroom suite at the hotel, which meant she would have her own bedroom, but she would still be in close proximity to the man. It's not as if he went into an office every day, either.

She prayed she wouldn't suddenly take up sleep-walking.

"SANDI WILL TAKE ME to the beach, won't she?" Patrick asked. "I think she likes the beach, don't you? You'll let her take me, won't you, Dad?"

Jack thought of the bikini Sandi wore that day. He wondered if she had a one-piece suit that covered her from neck to ankles. Maybe a nanny uniform would be a good idea, after all. Something shapeless that would hide her lovely figure. Hair in a bun. No makeup. Eyeglasses. The kind that hid half the face.

"Yes, she can take you to the beach," he said, absently adding, "Patrick, you know you're not supposed to jump on the bed."

He obligingly stopped and dropped cross-legged to the surface.

"Too bad we don't have a kitchen so she can bake cookies. Will we have a house soon so Sandi can make me cookies?"

"I didn't hire Sandi to bake cookies for you, Patrick," he reminded him. "She's going to look after you. She also said she'd show you the places boys your age like to go to."

Patrick grinned. "Cool."

"I also asked her to make sure you had some lessons this summer. Not to prepare you for kindergarten," he hurriedly added, "just to teach you things about Montgomery Beach."

Jack looked at his watch pointedly, then at his son. Patrick grimaced.

"Why do I need a bath? I went swimming."

"Not the same, slugger." He picked him up and swung him up into the air, then draped the boy over his shoulder. "Soap and hot water is very necessary to a clean body."

Within moments, Patrick was giggling as Jack drew his bath.

Jack always enjoyed times like this, which he called his "dad time." Patrick happily played with his tub toys and splashed his dad, while Jack worked to get him clean without ending up half soaked himself. A half hour later, Patrick was sleepy enough to allow himself to be dressed in his Snoopy pajamas and tucked into bed. Jack made sure the night-light was turned on and the bedroom door left ajar as he left the room. He stopped at the bar long enough to pour himself a snifter of brandy and head for the balcony.

He relaxed in a chair and lit up a cigar. He never smoked around Patrick and always smoked outside. This was his time to unwind and enjoy the peace and quiet of the evening.

As he looked out over the ocean with waves crashing onto the beach and then upward to the stars, he wondered if he could find a home that could give him the same relaxing view. As he sat there smoking and sipping his brandy, he could hear music coming from the lounge below. He recalled they offered dancing.

It would be easy enough to have a hotel baby-sitter

come in so he could go downstairs and have a drink down there. Maybe even meet someone.

Just as quickly as the idea formed in his mind, it disappeared.

Jack thought back over the past couple of months, when he began to realize his life was ready to take another turn. Patrick would be starting kindergarten in the fall, his business was growing faster than even he had forecasted and he didn't like the idea of his son growing up in an apartment. Even a luxury penthouse apartment in a secure building.

He wanted Patrick to have the kind of carefree childhood he'd had. He'd started thinking about finding a house in a small city outside of San Francisco that was close enough to the city for driving in if he had to, but far enough away where a small-town atmosphere still lingered.

When Dylan had called to tell him he was getting married and to ask him if he would be his best man, Jack saw it as a good chance to look over Montgomery Beach as a possible home base. He didn't waste any time checking out the schools, contacting a realtor Karl had recommended and seeing about relocating his office here. So far, all looked good.

Except that Mrs. Morrison wasn't interesting in moving with them, since she didn't want to be so far from her grandchildren. He'd hate losing her, but he understood.

Mrs. Montgomery had graciously offered to help him find a suitable housekeeper. He knew anyone Grace Montgomery recommended would be more than suitable. She had also offered to ensure Patrick's acceptance into the nearby private school, but Jack had explained he wanted him to attend a public school.

He'd officially started to panic when the older woman started talking about decorating services and landscaping firms. Did he want to hire a cook? How many maids would he require, and did he also want to hire a driver? She made relocating sound as if a major battle plan was required.

In San Francisco, he'd retained a cleaning service that came in twice a week for the heavy cleaning. Mrs. Morrison did the cooking, laundry and light cleaning, along with being there for Patrick. Jack preferred to drive himself everywhere. Patrick was required to keep his toys picked up in his room and to make his own bed.

Jack knew now that he wanted to make a home here in Montgomery Beach. In the back of his mind, he hoped that Sandi Galloway would help him make a start in that direction.

He idly blew several smoke rings and watched them drift upward until they dissipated.

He knew he'd hired Sandi because Patrick wanted her so badly. Even if he feared she was going to prove the kind of distraction he didn't need. Even with her wearing that sexy bikini today, he knew she was the kind of woman who deserved a husband and children of her own.

That kind of life wasn't something Jack was about to give any woman.

"SHE'S GOING TO HAVE breakfast with us, right?" Patrick's voice was muffled as he pulled his favorite Batman T-shirt over his head.

"Right." Jack helped him pull it down the rest of the way. He was relieved to see that his son chose dark blue shorts to go with his bright red shirt. He usually chose clashing colors that jarred the eyes.

The little boy suddenly ran over to the dresser and pulled out a pair of turquoise cotton shorts. "Maybe these will look nicer."

"No, what you have on is fine," his father hurriedly assured him, amused by his son's sudden interest in his grooming.

Patrick rushed into the bathroom and brushed his teeth, then attacked his unruly hair with a brush. Jack was impressed. It was usually a battle to get him to brush his hair and teeth.

"Can I use some of your good smelly stuff?" he asked.

"You don't need it, kiddo." Jack turned when he heard a knock at the door. "Sounds like she's here."

"I'll get it!" Patrick raced out of his room and toward the door, with Jack following at a slower pace. "Sandi!" He launched himself at her, throwing his arms around her waist.

"Now this is the kind of greeting I like," she laughed, hugging him back. She looked over his head at Jack, her smile still there. "Mr. O'Connor."

"Jack," he insisted. "We're very informal here, Sandi. Let me help you with those." He moved forward and grabbed one of her suitcases. "I'm going to begin house hunting, so hopefully we won't be in these cramped quarters for too much longer."

Sandi thought of her bedroom at the bungalow that was maybe a fourth of the size of the suite's living room. "True, we wouldn't want to suffer, would we?" she said. "I do hate it when rooms are no larger than the average house. You can't spread out and relax, can you?"

Jack grinned at her tongue-in-cheek reply as he led the way. "This is your room." He set her suitcase on the rack in front of the king-size bed. "If there's anything you need, just call Housekeeping. Are you ready for breakfast?"

She nodded as she looked around the room. "Definitely."

"I want French toast," Patrick announced as they left the suite. "And bacon. And juice."

"And milk," Jack added playfully, yet sternly. For now, he knew it was better he concentrate on Patrick than on Sandi. Especially her bare legs beneath her short denim skirt. She was dressed simply, in the denim skirt and a pale green T-shirt that had lace edging on the rounded neckline. Her tan sandals revealed toes painted a pastel green that almost matched her T-shirt. She'd pulled her hair back into a ponytail that bounced with every step she took. As they walked down the hallway, her head was bent as she listened to Patrick's excited chatter and replied when given a chance.

"Dad said when we get a house, I can have a puppy," he announced. "And maybe a kitten so the puppy will have someone to play with. I couldn't have one in our apartment, cuz it wouldn't be fair for them. We didn't have a backyard," he confided.

She hid her smile. "It's true. A cat and dog need a backyard."

She shot Jack a look filled with amusement as they entered the elevator. "They could prove to be an interesting combination if they stay true to their species."

Jack punched the button for the lobby. "Think I

should add some fish and maybe a couple of mice to the food chain?''

Patrick looked up at the adults, looking from one to the other. ''What's a food chain?''

''Apples and oranges and bananas,'' Sandi said easily, earning a silent ''thank you'' from Jack, who knew Patrick wouldn't appreciate hearing that, if given a chance, the cat would happily eat the fish and mice. ''Another food chain is pork, beef and chicken.''

When they reached the restaurant, Jack spoke to the hostess, while Patrick ran toward the large saltwater aquarium set up by the entrance. Sandi watched him, making sure he didn't wander any farther but that he was still out of earshot.

''I generally believe in telling the truth to my students no matter what question they ask,'' she explained. ''But I didn't think this question deserved a truthful answer.''

''I've told him it wouldn't be a good idea to get a kitten along with the puppy, but he's afraid the puppy will be lonely while he's at school,'' Jack explained. ''The problem is, I'm afraid he'll suddenly decide it might be a good idea to get two puppies.''

Sandi grinned. ''Then I suggest you only look at small or medium dogs. Some of them are great with kids.''

Jack looked over to where Patrick had his nose pressed against the glass watching the fish with avid fascination.

''You know, it's amazing. One day I was holding this tiny creature in my arms, even though I was so afraid I'd drop him. He was barely an hour old, his face all red and purple as he howled his displeasure at the world. I was positive I'd screw up somehow with him. Now I look at him and I find it hard to remember that little guy I held in my arms,'' he said quietly.

"I've always enjoyed watching kids during that time when their personalities start to develop,'' Sandi said. "They become individuals then.''

"If you end up with Patrick for a student in the fall, you'll certainly have your hands full,'' Jack warned.

She lowered her voice. "Ah, but you forget, I'll have him all summer. That will give me plenty of time to brainwash him into becoming the perfect child. Parents will hate you for having a child who does everything right while theirs run around acting like wild animals.''

He shook his head and chuckled. "Good luck.''

"Are we gonna eat or what?'' Patrick demanded as he hopped back to them. "I'm starving!''

"Do you get the idea that your child is afraid he'll expire in the next five minutes if he isn't fed?'' Sandi murmured, even as the hostess gestured for them to follow her.

"He's like that with every meal.''

Sandi sensed Jack close behind her as they walked to the booth the hostess indicated. Maybe she didn't smell coconut oil on him, but whatever he was wearing was just as good, if not better. Patrick waited until she slid across the leather seat before he sat next to her. He smiled and said, "Thank you,'' when the hostess handed him the children's menu.

Later, as Patrick attacked his French toast and bacon, Jack discussed Sandi's duties with her.

"A gas credit card, written permission for medical treatment in case I can't be reached, a key to the suite and a cell phone,'' he explained, handing her a small padded manila envelope. "There are times when that can happen, since I'll be off looking for office space, so I can start moving down my files. Not to mention, finding a house."

"I doubt you'll have any problem finding office space," Sandi said, sipping her coffee. "A lot of small businesses have been moving down here, so there's quite a few office complexes on the outskirts of town. How does your staff feel about you relocating the business?"

Jack chuckled. "My staff consists of an administrative assistant, a receptionist and two researchers who work part-time while they're going to college. My AA is moving down here, and I helped my receptionist find a new job, which, she enjoyed telling me, pays more than what I was paying her." Predictably, Sandi chuckled. "And my researchers can still work for me via fax and e-mail."

"You sound as if you've had this planned for some time."

"I think it's been in the back of my mind for a while, but when Dylan called me about his wedding, and I realized Patrick would be attending kindergarten in the fall, I decided it was time to do something about getting out of the city," he replied. He looked up and smiled his thanks when the waitress refilled his coffee cup. "The plan was to get us settled down here over the summer, so that Patrick would have a chance to meet some kids his own age and feel more comfortable about attending school in the fall."

"Kindergarten will be so cool!" Patrick piped up, waving his fork around.

When Jack pointed to his plate, he immediately

stabbed another syrup-laden piece of French toast and brought it to his mouth...before opening it to speak.

"Chew, swallow, then speak," Jack reminded him.

Sandi enjoyed seeing the obviously strong bond between father and son. Jack never talked down to the boy, and appeared to be strict when it was necessary. And Patrick seemed to accept his dad's rules with no argument. She was positive Patrick would try to push his boundaries every so often. It was natural for any child his age, and Patrick seemed to want to go as far as he could. She honestly hoped she would have him in her class in the fall, because she knew he would offer a lot of challenges, which she would do her best to meet.

"Karl said you grew up here," Jack commented.

She nodded. "Our parents had a card and stationery store until they retired five years ago and sold the store. It used to be in the plaza near Karl's shop. Over time, most of their business expanded into creating wedding and party invitations. They even hired a calligrapher for custom invitations."

"Do they still live here in Montgomery Beach?"

"No, they're traveling the country in an RV. Right now, they're driving through Kansas. Mom said it really is flat. They plan to visit all fifty states. I reminded them they won't be able to take the RV to Hawaii, so they're checking out the other forty-nine first."

"An RV is like one of those really big campers, huh?" Patrick asked.

"Pretty much," she replied. "They even have a satellite dish on it so my dad won't miss his favorite shows. They also meet a lot of the same people at various campsites, so they've made friends along the way. But that doesn't mean they can get out of calling

Steffi and me every week to let us know they're okay. And they'll be back for Steffi's wedding."

"Wow." Patrick's eyes shone. "I bet it's like camping out."

"Yes, but without the creepy crawlies in a sleeping bag, and no leaky tents." She wrinkled her nose with distaste. "That was never my favorite part of camping."

"No roasting hot dogs over a campfire, no telling ghost stories," Jack added.

"Can we go camping, Dad?" Patrick pleaded. "I wanna have that kind of fun."

"Why don't we get settled in a house before we start planning field trips," Jack advised, signing the check. "I've got to go back upstairs and make some calls." He looked at Sandi. "I gather you have plans."

Sandi nodded. "If it's all right with you, I thought I'd take Patrick over to the play park." She smiled at the boy, who bounced up and down in excitement. "I'm sure we can find plenty to do there. We probably won't be back until this afternoon."

"That sounds good to me." Jack stood up and brought up the rear as they left the restaurant. He inclined his head in Sandi's direction. "I trust you with my son, Sandi," he said quietly before he walked on.

She watched him walk away, not looking at all like a wealthy financier in his worn black jeans and a dark blue polo shirt. But it didn't stop womens' eyes from watching him with undisguised interest. More than one tried her best to catch his eye, but all failed. Sandi felt more than a twinge of pleasure that he didn't flirt. An inner voice reminded her that he might not do anything with his son in the vicinity, but she quickly silenced it.

"How about a pit stop, then we'll head for the play park," she suggested.

"What's a pit stop?" he asked.

"A guy term for the bathroom."

Patrick giggled. "I like guy terms."

"Of course you do. You're a guy, aren't you?"

Sandi was glad she'd reacquainted herself with the facilities available for children. She hoped that by taking Patrick around town, he would have a chance to meet children his age and make a few friends before he started school. She knew that while he was excited about beginning kindergarten, a part of him had to be apprehensive, too. If he'd stayed in San Francisco, he would be attending kindergarten with children he already knew. He'd be in familiar surroundings. She was determined to spend this summer helping him settle in.

What had started out as a playground when Sandi and Steffi were little girls had expanded to now include a miniature golf course, a go-cart track, bumper boats, water slides, batting cages, a roller hockey rink and baseball diamond. There was even a pizza parlor next to the complex that catered to lots of birthday parties.

Sandi parked by the playground and helped Patrick out of the back seat.

"This is so neat!" His dark eyes shone with excitement as he gazed over the acres filled with every imaginable idea of fun available for a child. "Was this here when you were little?" He took her hand as they crossed the parking lot.

"Not all of it. We just had the playground," she said. "But my sister and I were down here every weekend fighting over who would go down the slide first and who could swing the highest.''

"Did you always win?"

"No, Steffi cheated," she confided in a hushed voice. "She's eight minutes older than I am, so she was always bossy."

"I wish I had a brother." His voice turned wistful. "I asked Dad if I could have a brother, but he said it's not very easy to have one."

"Maybe once you move down here he'll change his mind and give you one." She slipped off her sandals when they reached the sand where the playground equipment was set up. Children of all ages were running everywhere. The sounds of their excited screams echoed in the air.

Patrick hopped onto a swing while Sandi walked around behind him and began pushing him. He squealed with delight as he flew higher and higher.

Sandi could see this nanny business was going to be a piece of cake.

JACK SPENT THE MORNING on the phone to clients and his office staff and reading scrolls of figures on his computer monitor.

"You have nothing to worry about with those investments, Harry," he assured a frantic-sounding man as he studied the figures on the monitor. He quickly changed the screen to a graph and charted what he'd just read. "Have I steered you wrong yet?"

"No, but there's always a first time."

"Harry, if I felt there could be any problem, I would pull you out immediately. Tell your wife she can have those emerald earrings she found."

"Earrings? Now she wants a necklace and ring to go with them!"

Jack laughed as he rang off. He made a few more notes, sent a fax to his assistant and turned off his computer. When he glanced at the clock, he was stunned to see it was late afternoon. He'd barely stopped for lunch, only taking time to order a quick salad from room service in between calls.

He was munching on an apple when the telephone rang. He was tempted to let his voice mail pick up, but for all he knew it could be Sandi.

"Jack, how are you doing, dear?"

He winced. He wished he had let it go to voice mail. "I'm doing fine, Grace. How about you?"

"Still trying to make sense of everything that happened, but it's clear that Dylan loves Whitney in a way that he never did Cori, so I hope he'll be happy," she replied. "Harriet is staying with me for a while."

Jack stiffened at her announcement. He refused to believe it could be an innocent comment. He didn't want to think what it could mean.

"But that isn't why I called. I heard of an excellent nanny, who will be available within the next few days. The family is moving back east, and she doesn't care to move with them. I understand she's a real treasure, and the children she is looking after now are in Patrick's age range."

"Thank you for thinking of me, Grace, but I just hired someone. A kindergarten teacher, no less, and Patrick is very happy with her." He sat back down at the desk and idly doodled on his notepad.

"Really? I hadn't heard of a teacher looking for a nanny position."

"Actually she wasn't, but since she's free for the

summer, I thought I'd offer her the position. Her name is Sandi Galloway. Her sister runs a catering business.''

"Oh, yes, Stefanie Galloway. A lovely young woman. She's getting married soon. Both are lovely girls.''

Jack could hear a slight hesitation in Grace's voice. He was curious as to why it was there, but he didn't want to come right out and ask, thereby giving in to her need to tell him.

"I'm afraid I have to go, Grace. They'll be back soon. Sandi took him over to the play park."

"The Country Club also offers some excellent childrens' activities," she informed him. "I know it would just be a formality to obtain a membership for you. I'm sure you could pick up some new clients there, while Patrick meets the right kind of children."

"Thanks, Grace, but I've never had the patience to play golf and right now I'm not looking for new clients," he replied.

"If the Galloway woman doesn't work out, let me know and I'll see if Christina is still available," she offered. "Although I doubt she'll be unemployed for long. Nannies with her qualifications are very rare. I swear they're worth their weight in gold nowadays."

Jack recognized her ploy and refused to give in. "I'm sure that's true. Goodbye, Grace."

He'd barely hung up the phone before the door burst open and Patrick raced into the room. He fairly leaped into his dad's lap.

His face was red, his hair flying every which way and his clothes were filthy.

Jack doubted he'd ever seen his son looking happier.

Chapter Four

"This is the best day I ever had, Dad! It was so cool!" Patrick shouted, leaping into his father's arms. "Sandi took me to the playground, and she pushed me on the swings until my feet touched the sky. Then we went on the slide and on a merry-go-round, but it's not the kind of merry-go-round that has horses and funny music. This one you have to push around and Sandi made it go really fast." He talked so fast he had to stop to take a breath. "Then we played on the dinosaurs they had there. I sat on a trikertops," he stumbled over the word.

"Triceratops," she murmured.

Patrick's eyes glowed. "It was really big." He held his arms out for emphasis.

"I gather you enjoyed yourself," Jack chuckled, looking over his son's shorts and T-shirt that were caked with dirt.

Sandi shrugged when she noticed the direction of his gaze. "Boys and dirt just seem to go together. Nothing that soap and water can't fix," she assured him in a breezy tone. "Along with some hard scrubbing."

"A bath?" Patrick's head swiveled around so he

could see Sandi. He looked as if she'd just uttered the direst of threats. "I have to take a bath? But I had one last night!"

"Obviously there's a boy here who thinks a bath is a fate worse than death," Sandi said lightly, tapping the tip of his nose with her finger. "Don't worry, m'boy, you haven't taken a bath my way. You'll change your mind in no time and look forward to having a bath."

Jack let Patrick slide down to his feet. "I can give him his bath," he offered, familiar with his son's aversion to soap and water.

"Don't worry, I have a plan," she confided with a bright smile.

"But I'm hungry!" he wailed.

"Then you'll get clean all the faster, won't you?" Jack teased.

"You'll love this bath, trust me," she told the boy as she guided him toward the bathroom. She looked over her shoulder at Jack. "It will probably take some doing to coax him out of the tub."

"No, it won't!" could be heard from Patrick.

She laughed. "We'll be out in a half hour or so."

Jack settled in a chair with his *Wall Street Journal* but kept his ear tuned to the bathroom for Patrick's predictable noisy protests. At first, all he heard was the sound of water running into the bathtub and his son's giggles. It took him awhile to realize that he hadn't heard one argument from Patrick about bathing. In fact, if he wasn't mistaken, Patrick was actually laughing and Sandi was laughing along with him. Unable to contain his curiosity, he put his newspaper aside and got up.

He stopped inside the bedroom where he could see

past the bathroom door without their seeing him. Bubbles surrounded Patrick in the tub. Jack recalled that even bubble baths hadn't made the boy happy. Except these bubbles were bright blue. Patrick was occupied drawing pictures on the tile wall with chunky green, red and purple crayons. His face bore colorful designs of the same colors.

"If you've got to wash with soap, you might as well use soap crayons," he could hear Sandi tell Patrick as she used a red soap crayon on his hair. "That way, you can draw all the pictures you want on the walls and wipe them clean." She lathered his hair, then styled the sudsy strands until they stood up straight. She held a mirror in front of Patrick. "What do you think?"

He howled with laughter. "I look funny!"

"Of course, you do. You're supposed to look funny." She leaned forward and drew a purple beard on Patrick's chin. "Now it's up to you to get all that off so we can go eat."

He looked unhappy to hear his playtime was nearing an end.

"You're hungry, remember?" she teased, trailing a small pail in the water then urging him to lean forward so she could rinse the suds off his back.

"Can we play with the crayons again?" he asked.

"They're the best way to get clean." She held up a towel and wrapped it around him as he stepped out of the tub.

Jack could feel an odd sensation within his body as he watched Sandi briskly rub Patrick dry then wield a hair dryer on the boy's hair. He carefully backed his way out of the room and back into the small living room. When Sandi and Patrick later came out, he was seated in the chair with the *Wall Street Journal* in his hands. If asked, he wouldn't have been able to recall one word he'd read.

Patrick was squeaky-clean and looking happier after a bath than Jack had ever seen him. At some point, Sandi had slipped off to her own room and changed into a yellow gingham sundress and pulled her hair up in a saucy ponytail decorated with a yellow gingham ribbon, the ends dangling down. He couldn't miss the gold ankle bracelet emphasizing a dainty ankle, or that her toenails were painted a yellow that matched her dress.

He suddenly decided yellow was his favorite color.

"Any special preference for dinner?" he asked.

"As long as it isn't sushi, I'm not fussy," she said.

"That's too bad, because sushi is Patrick's favorite," he said glibly.

"Sushi?" Patrick made a face. "Gross! I don't even like fish when it's cooked. Can we have barbecue ribs?"

Jack looked at Sandi.

"Hey, I'm just the hired help," she laughed, holding up her hands. "Food is food. I can even go over to my sister's and mooch off her. You don't need to provide my meals."

"Then barbecue ribs it is, and there is absolutely no reason why you can't come with us. Someone has to keep the kid, here, clean," Jack said, ushering them out the door. As she passed by him, he was aware of a light scent emanating from her skin. "And Sandi—" his voice dropped to a husky whisper "—you are far from the hired help in my eyes."

He smiled briefly as he noticed the instant flush coloring her cheeks. Obviously she was as aware of him as he was of her.

SANDI WAS AFRAID she could easily fall into that cliché of the nanny infatuated with her employer. She thought of all the gothic romances she'd read as a teenager that had the young naive governess or nanny fall deeply in love with the dark and brooding master of the house. Just because a majority of them were set a hundred years ago didn't mean it couldn't still happen. She was single. He was single. And very good-looking. The only difference was, they weren't sequestered in a drafty old house with him being all dark, arrogant and brooding, while a stern housekeeper hovered in the background.

She quickly reined in her imagination before it soared out of control. As a kindergarten teacher, having an overactive imagination was a good thing. As a nanny with a sexy-looking boss, having one was very dangerous to the libido.

Jack's silver Jaguar sedan was as comfortable and unassuming as Jack. She was surprised when he pulled into the parking lot of a well-known restaurant popular for its barbecue offerings.

"Patrick inherited my plebeian taste in food," he said as they crossed the parking lot with Patrick walking between them. "We're a lot happier going out for a burger than having a five-course meal."

"You can't tell me you don't like caviar?" she mocked.

Jack made a face eerily like his son's when sushi had been mentioned. "Give me a greasy cheeseburger piled high with onions any day."

"But only if antacids come as a side order," Sandi quipped.

The moment Jack opened the door, country western music rolled out over them, along with the tangy aroma of spicy barbecue sauce mixed with beef and pork. Sandi could feel her taste buds salivating at the prospect of the kind of food that left you wanting more.

Sandi enjoyed watching Patrick as they were seated in a booth in one corner of the busy restaurant. She was sure that the boy ate out a great deal, but he seemed to act as if it was a special treat for him. She watched him look around as if he wanted to see everything going on.

"He was always a people watcher," Jack said, noting her interest. "I told him he'll make a great cop someday."

"Arrest the bad guys and use a siren." Patrick mimicked the sound of a siren until he caught his father's chastising eye. He quickly sat up straight and made the motion of zipping his mouth shut.

"I don't know why you need a nanny when he's this well behaved," Sandi told Jack.

"Believe me, he's not this well behaved all the time. I think he's trying to impress you, but, sooner or later, his true personality will emerge," Jack said ruefully. "That's when he wants everything his own way. And can be pretty sneaky about it, too."

"Don't worry, I've dealt with some miniature con men in my time." She grinned at Patrick, who was now listening to their conversation with rapt attention.

His brow furrowed in thought. "What's a con man?"

"Little boys who think they can always get their way," she teased as she opened her menu.

"I don't always get my way." He pouted. "Daddy wouldn't get me that new video game I want."

"Not when it's meant for someone a good ten years older than you," Jack pointed out. "Even then, I think it was a bit much for a teenager. Besides, you should be outside playing instead of indoors playing with your computer."

Patrick tipped his head to one side and studied his father. "But shouldn't I have a backyard to play in? And a puppy to play with?"

Jack looked at Sandi. "See what I mean?" He turned back to his son. "Don't worry, the time will come when you'll be bored playing in your own yard. Junior ribs for you?"

Patrick nodded. "And fries and Coke."

"Fries and milk." Jack looked at Sandi questioningly when the waiter appeared by their table.

"A regular order of beef ribs with the beans and coleslaw, please," she said. "And iced tea to drink."

After Jack placed his and Patrick's orders, he turned back to Sandi. He placed his folded hands on the table as he tossed out his challenge.

"Okay, teach, give us an idea of what a day in your class is like."

"Let's see." She tapped her forefinger against her chin. "There's naptime in the cages, of course, though we *have* come up with lighter chains to keep them tied together."

Patrick looked from one to the other. "But I thought you got to play in kindergarten." A hint of a panicked whimper was in his voice.

Sandi leaned over and ruffled Patrick's hair. "I'm

teasing, Patrick. In kindergarten there are counting games, spelling games, music and art classes sometimes. In my last class, we had a hamster named Fido and a parakeet named Squeaks.'' She shrugged when she noticed Jack's amusement. ''Don't even ask. I let the kids name the hamster. They decided he'd be the dog they really wanted but couldn't have in the class.''

''Can my class have a dog?'' Patrick asked hopefully.

''Unfortunately dogs and schools don't mix, Patrick,'' she explained.

He frowned in thought. ''Then how come they have schools for dogs?''

''Yeah, teach, how come they have schools for dogs?'' Jack grinned widely.

Sandi looked from one to the other. ''You two are enjoying this, aren't you?'' she asked, narrowing her eyes in suspicion.

Jack looked at Patrick, then the two looked at Sandi with identical looks of pure innocence.

''We merely asked you a question, Sandi,'' Jack said with deceptive smoothness.

Rescued by the waiter's appearance with their meals, she breathed a sigh of relief.

''Don't worry, we can discuss it further after we've eaten,'' Jack said with a wicked smile that did strange things to the pit of her stomach.

She reminded herself that in real life nannies didn't fantasize about their bosses, but then, she'd never been a nanny before. She should have stuck to waitressing for the summer. With her twin for her boss, she didn't have these kind of worries. With Steffi, all she had to worry about was not breaking any dishes and not swiping any of the food during a social function. Of course, she did feel strangled when she wore the bow tie and the starched shirt itched.

If she wanted to cast the blame even further, she could blame Doug for being a member of a lower life-form. For getting engaged to his boss's daughter because he felt the alliance would cement his slot in the law firm where he worked. For letting her think he was furthering his career by working late when he was really out partying with *her*. For letting her think he was doing it all for their future. Oh sure, more like his and Miss Saline-Implants-and-Liposuction's future.

Sandi didn't care what anyone said, she just knew nothing about that woman was natural. Her daddy probably paid a pretty penny to get his daughter that kind of body. She was so lost in her thoughts, she didn't notice Jack watching her with a narrowed gaze as he ate his own dinner.

It was a good thing she didn't notice, because the heat in his gaze might have worried her.

"I'd say you were one hungry munchkin," Sandi said, congratulating Patrick on his empty plate.

He beamed. "I like ribs."

"I can see that."

"And when I have a dog, I can take the bones home, so he'll have something, too."

Sandi glanced at Jack, who was grimacing.

"A big dog." Patrick held his arms out as far as they would go.

"Check, please," Jack's voice was strangled.

"You shouldn't think about what kind of dog you want, Patrick," she advised.

"Why not?"

"Because you should let the dog choose you. If you do that, your dog will always be your friend. You can say you want a big dog, but it might be a little dog who chooses you to be his best friend. Unless, of course—'' she cast a glance at Jack ''—your father is going to talk to various breeders.''

He shook his head. ''Patrick and I already decided that if there was going to be a dog in the house, we'd go to the animal shelter and look for a dog that truly needed a home. A pedigree isn't all that necessary to a kid who just wants someone to roll around with.''

''A boy is dog's best friend,'' she stated, paraphrasing a popular phrase.

Jack took care of the check and, once outside, Sandi took a deep breath of the tangy air.

''You don't really think of salt air and barbecue going together, but it seems to work,'' she said as they walked to Jack's car. As she sat in the passenger seat, she again enjoyed the rich aroma of leather. From Jack's attitude—or lack thereof—she suspected that he didn't see his car as a status symbol, but merely a form of transportation. He drove as easily as he seemed to do everything else.

She knew she shouldn't be aware of him as a man. It was very dangerous. For both her senses and her job.

Not to mention, while he wouldn't mind a dog without a pedigree for his son, she was pretty sure the woman in his life would require a pedigree a mile long. She could easily visualize the type of women Jack dated, and she wouldn't be surprised if they all resembled Miss Saline-Implants-and-Liposuction, but, hopefully, with some smarts thrown in.

Sandi knew the last thing she needed in her life right now was a man. Even thinking about one was dangerous.

Except she wasn't about to allow Doug's defection to ruin her life. She wouldn't wish them a happy life. That much of a good sport she wasn't. Now a maid would pick up Doug's dirty underwear off the bathroom floor and clean the dried globs of toothpaste off the bathroom sink. Someone else would make sure his coffee was brewed just right and only Jif smooth peanut butter touched his lips. She'd always been a Skippy crunchy fan herself.

All in all, she was much better off without him. All she had to do was remember that when she felt blue.

PATRICK WAS NOTICEABLY drooping as they crossed the spacious lobby to the elevators. When they entered an empty car, he leaned against Sandi while his eyelids closed with weariness.

"I don't think there will be any argument about going to bed tonight," Jack murmured, looking down at his son.

Sandi smiled. She had slipped her arm around Patrick's shoulders. "Well, he did have a very busy day today. He ran nonstop around the playground because he didn't want to miss anything."

"Don't wanna go to bed," the boy mumbled with eyes closed fully now. "Not tired. Wanna go ride the bumper boats."

Jack reached for the boy and hoisted him up against his shoulder. Patrick sleepily circled his dad's neck with his arms and with a soft sigh, rested his cheek against his shoulder. As they stepped off the elevator, they passed one couple who smiled at the boy sleeping comfortably in his dad's arms.

"What's scary is, he'll wake up tomorrow with all

circuits on turbo power.'' Jack gestured for Sandi to open the door for them.

She preceded him into Patrick's bedroom and turned on the night-light sitting on the chest of drawers near the door. The lamp sent a soft glow throughout the room as she pulled a pair of pajamas out of one drawer. Within a few minutes she had Patrick undressed and under the covers.

''How about a glass of wine?'' Jack asked when Sandi left Patrick's room. She'd left the door slightly ajar so they could hear Patrick if he happened to call out.

She hesitated.

He smiled. ''Come on. You deserve one after your first day on the job. White or red?'' He held up two bottles.

''White. Red always puts me to sleep.''

''And that's a bad thing?'' he gently teased, as he poured wine into a glass and handed it to her.

She accepted the glass and followed him outside on to the balcony. She took the chair he offered and sat down with her full skirt billowing out around her ankles.

Jack tried not to look at the ankle bracelet that seemed to taunt him under the soft light.

''You and Patrick seemed to have already struck up a good rapport,'' he commented from his chair next to hers, sipping his wine. ''I'm glad for that. He likes the idea of moving here because it's something new. I was afraid once the plan sunk in, he might not find it as fascinating. He has lots of friends in San Francisco, and I know he'll miss them. Assuring him they can always come to visit isn't enough. Not at that age.''

"He met a few boys his age today, which was a good start. The more we go back to the playground, the more he'll meet. I'm sure he'll even meet ones who will be attending his school, perhaps be in his class," she assured him. "You don't have to worry about Patrick. He's an outgoing friendly little boy. He'll do just fine."

Jack smiled and held his glass out in a toast. "Praise a father always enjoys hearing. Especially from someone who's had as much exposure to his age group as you have."

With a regal nod of the head, she touched her glass to his before she sipped her wine. "Give me a roomful of five-year-olds, and I'll tell you who will end up in the priesthood, who will end up as doctors, who will go into politics and who will end up on 'Cops.'"

"That is truly a gift," Jack said gravely.

"It's not just a gift, it's necessary." Sandi suddenly grinned. "I could tell you stories that would curl your hair."

"Yet you keep on teaching."

"Sure. How many jobs give you the summer off to play?" She stretched her legs out, propping her feet on a nearby small table. "For that matter, how many jobs let you play during work hours?"

"What did you usually do during your playtime?" he asked, curious about this multifaceted woman who fascinated him more every moment he knew her.

She shrugged. "Went camping. Took the train across Canada. Signed on with an archeological dig in Central America. One time I even worked as a companion for a very nice elderly widow who wanted to travel through Russia."

"Widow, huh? It sounds sedate."

"Sedate?" Sandi laughed. "Fran always led a pretty wild social life, and joining a tour group didn't slow her down one whit. I was the one falling into bed every night, while she wanted to explore the nightlife. One time she came in at 4:00 a.m. after a night of hitting the underground bars with an army colonel. By the time we got back to Seattle, I was ready for a rest home and she was planning an outback trek to Australia."

"And she didn't ask you to go along?"

"Yes, she did and I begged off. I told her she obviously needed someone a lot older with more energy. Instead she met a sheep rancher there and settled down with him." Her smile held fond memories. "I can only hope I have a fraction of Fran's energy when I'm her age."

"Sounds as if this summer could turn out more than a little boring for you," Jack commented.

Sandi shook her head. "It's not as if I've gone over Niagara Falls in a barrel. And I never would. I was able to join an archeological dig because the head archeologist was a neighbor. I chaperoned a group of high school juniors on a train trip and, believe me, they tested my sanity every minute of the day and night. On the camping trip, I got poison oak, a bad sunburn and had an allergic reaction to a bug bite that left me unable to sit down for almost two weeks. Looking after one boy, who actually listens to me, is pure pleasure." She used her wineglass to gesture toward the balcony railing. The sound of ocean waves crashing against the nearby rocks seemed to roar around them. "Not to mention that the view is heavenly. I've always been a water baby." She shifted in her chair so she could face Jack as she curled her legs up under her. "What about you? Lived in San Francisco all your life?"

He shook his head, unfazed that a mere employee was asking him personal questions that should be none of her business.

"San Diego actually, until I went away to college. I met Dylan and J.T. there and we came back here a lot for holidays and vacations. After I received my degree, I went on for my master's, then went to work for a financial corporation that transferred me to San Francisco about seven years ago. I went out on my own four years ago."

"That had to have taken a lot of guts and a lot of advance planning," she said softly. "You had a son to consider, which must make the fear of failure very real. What you do isn't exactly risk-free."

"Actually it was more dumb luck than anything," he admitted. "I had a client who liked what I did and told me I should go out on my own. He was willing to back me and even brought me a few clients. Luckily I succeeded for them, and I was able to operate in the black before my first year was over."

"Which means you like to take chances." Sandi narrowed her eyes in thought as she studied him in the moonlight, their only illumination.

Dressed casually in a black polo shirt and black jeans with his dark hair and finely honed features, he should have looked intimidating. But Sandi didn't find him the least bit so. Instead she found him downright sexy. Especially when they were sitting out here alone while seductive music from below floated upward. The crashing waves only added to the romantic setting.

She was treading on dangerous ground here and reminded herself she was here to work. Not think about her boss in a manner that was anything but business-like.

She wondered about Patrick's mother. While she wasn't averse to questioning Jack about himself, she held back inquiring about the woman who must have played an important part in his life at one time. She imagined that would be a taboo subject. Patrick hadn't even mentioned his mother and she, sensibly, hadn't asked. She didn't want the boy to think she cared about anything other than him.

She already knew Patrick's greatest wish was to have a mother. It didn't take a rocket scientist to see that while the son wanted a mother, the father had no desire to take a wife.

"I'll be up early to make calls to London and Hong Kong," Jack said abruptly. "But I plan on looking at some houses in the afternoon. Why don't you and Patrick come along?"

"Kids and house hunting don't usually go hand in hand," she warned. "He'll be easily bored."

"We can tell him he'll need to check out the back-yard for his puppy."

"And what am I needed for?"

Jack's eyes bore into Sandi's for what seemed hours before he replied. "The most important aspect of house hunting—a woman's point of view."

She tore her eyes away and rose to her feet.

"I'll take Patrick to the playground until lunch then," she stated briskly. "Good night."

"Good night, Sandi."

She headed for her bedroom, unsure if her legs would hold her.

"He's playing with the hired help," she muttered as she brushed her teeth. "It's just a game with him," she continued as she pulled on her nightgown. "And I'm just going through some weird cycle. On the rebound from Doug, that's all it is."

Until she fell asleep, Sandi came up with countless reasons why Jack affected her so deeply. Even if she tried to blame it on the cycles of the moon, her own cycle and anything else that struck her fancy, she knew she was only lying to herself.

Jack O'Connor was a man no red-blooded woman could ignore, and Sandi most definitely was a woman of the red-blooded variety.

Chapter Five

"We can really eat breakfast this way?" Patrick asked Sandi as they walked through the plaza near the hotel.

"Why not?" She speared a cube of cantaloupe and lifted it to his lips. He grinned and snapped his teeth over the plastic fork, pulling the fruit off the tines. "You have your fresh fruit, your dairy—" she held up a container of yogurt "—fiber," she used her fork to gesture to the French baguette Patrick carried. "This is breakfast alfresco. Eating out in the open air," she clarified for him. "It's very continental."

"I like it," he said happily, skipping alongside her.

"And what are you two up to this beautiful morning?"

The duo stopped in front of the tux shop where Karl stood outside the glass door.

"We're having breakfast in fresca," Patrick informed him with self-importance.

Karl smiled. "Yes, I can see that. And it appears you have everything you require for your outdoor breakfast."

Sandi held up two sports bottles. "Orange juice," she explained. "We're going down to the beach to have our feast before we go to the playground."

He nodded. "It looks as if you two get along very well."

"Patrick is the man for me, even if he is a little short," she confided in a mock whisper. "But, I figure if I feed him a lot of healthy food, he'll shoot up a couple feet or so. Plus, I've got him at that trainable age. By the time he's an adult, he'll be just right."

Karl's chuckle blended with Patrick's giggle.

"Sandi is so funny," the boy told him between giggles. "She told the man at the juice bar that I was her main squeeze."

"And he is." She gathered him against her side and squeezed him to prove her point. "I may only have him for the summer, but it will be time enough to turn him into the perfect male."

Patrick walked over to the window and stared at the white dinner jacket hanging from a mahogany hanger set on a brass stand.

"How come we didn't wear somethin' like that to the wedding?" he asked, pointing at the jacket.

"Because that is called a dinner jacket. They are usually worn to formal dinners or cocktail parties," Karl explained.

"Dad's gotta get married before I grow up too much and can't wear my tuxedo," he whispered.

"I wouldn't worry, young Patrick. Your father told you he will buy you a new tuxedo when you outgrow the one you have now."

"Yeah, well, he's gotta do it before I start school." Patrick shifted his glance in Sandi's direction for a split second. "She can bake cookies," he confided in a whisper.

Karl crouched down so he was more on Patrick's

level. "That is very important for a mother, isn't it?" he whispered back.

The boy's head bobbed up and down.

"Dad's takin' us lookin' at houses after lunch. Sandi gets to help, too." He grinned. "Just like a real family."

Karl smiled. "Did you know if you wish for something hard enough, it can come true?"

Patrick was awed, as if he heard the answer to all his prayers.

"Hey, honey bear, are we having our breakfast alfresco or not?" Sandi called out.

"I'm comin'!" Patrick and Karl exchanged a look filled with conspiracy. "Then I'm gonna wish really hard." He took off running.

Sandi waved over her shoulder at Karl as she and Patrick walked away. Karl remained by the door until they were out of sight.

"I knew they would be perfect together," he murmured, boasting a self-satisfied smile. "Now Jack needs to realize the same thing and all will be well."

AFTER SANDI AND PATRICK finished their breakfast on the beach, they ended up staying there, digging for sand crabs and feeding bread crumbs to the seagulls. A walk along the shoreline had them discovering a tide pool, so Sandi gave an impromptu science lecture about the tiny occupants in the pool. Patrick was disappointed not to find any large crabs inhabiting a shell or anything resembling a sea monster, even though he did find a small sand dollar that was still intact. He carefully wrapped it in a napkin and slipped it into his shorts' pocket.

"Can we look for tide pools again?" he asked as they returned to the hotel.

"Of course, we can," she said promptly. "And each time we find one, you'll see something different."

"Cool."

They were so engrossed in their hunt for tide pools that they lost track of time.

When they stepped into the hotel suite, they found Jack seated in a chair reading a business magazine. He looked cool and comfortable in khaki pants and a white cotton shirt with the sleeves rolled up to his elbows. He arched an eyebrow in silent question at their sandy attire and bare feet.

"Sorry, boss, but yours isn't near as intimidating as the look the manager gave us when we walked through the lobby," Sandi told him. "I think he wished we had found a back way to sneak in."

Jack looked grim. He put his magazine to one side and stood up. "Did he say anything to you?"

"He asked Sandi if we were staying here," Patrick piped up. "Then she looked at him like she was a mean teacher and he was a bad student and told him of course we were. She said if he had a problem with that, he was to talk to you. The man got really nice then."

Jack turned to her.

She shrugged it off. "No big deal. Anyone with the name Chester has to show some attitude so his underlings will be afraid of him. Plus, some guests like the idea of a snobbish manager. Makes them feel important."

"Not around me they don't." He glanced at them.

"Why don't you two get cleaned up and we'll grab a quick lunch before we meet the realtor."

Sandi herded Patrick into his bedroom and closed the door.

Jack stared at the closed door for a moment then picked up the phone. His call was brief and to the point. After he finished his call, he knew the manager would never give Sandi and Patrick any grief again.

When Sandi left her bedroom, she'd changed out of her sandy attire and into a rose pink and white print cotton skirt that floated around her calves and a hip skimming rose pink cotton top with three large white buttons just below the round neckline. Her white ballerina style flats didn't give Jack a chance to find out if her toenails matched her outfit. She carried a straw hat in one hand. She looked as cool as a breath of spring and as delectable as a bowl of raspberry sherbet.

A part of Jack wondered if anyone would believe him if he introduced her as his son's nanny, since she so clearly didn't look the part. Another part asked why he should care. Still another part piped up that he should just relax and enjoy the view.

"PATRICK, ARE YOU SURE you won't be too bored while we talk to the realtor?" Jack asked his son, who sat comfortably in the back seat with his Game Boy.

"Huh?" He didn't look up from the game he was playing.

"Guess he won't," he murmured.

"Not as long as he gets to pronounce the suitability of the backyard as a play area," Sandi said.

"The realtor I spoke to said he can show us two

houses this afternoon,'' he told her. "I thought two would be more than enough with Patrick along.''

"Only if you're lucky and like the first one right off the bat.'' She kept her hat settled in her lap.

Jack noticed her scent was as springtime as her clothing. Her hair was pulled back in a French braid again, with a pink ribbon securing the ends. With her long skirt and almost-prim-looking top, she should have looked innocent. In his mind, she looked anything but. He was sorry the realtor would be along. He was even sorrier when it turned out the realtor and Sandi knew each other.

"Sandi Galloway?'' the man greeted her with a laugh and hug. "You look fantastic! Are you back for the summer?''

"You look pretty good yourself, Dennis. I'm here for good now. I'll be teaching kindergarten at Richards Elementary in the fall.''

"Really? You might have my daughter then. She starts there in the fall.''

Jack smiled. Good, he's married.

Sandi beamed. "You have kids then?''

Dennis grimaced. "Every other weekend. I've been divorced for about a year now.''

Jack's smile disappeared as quickly as it appeared.

"Are we gonna look at the houses?'' Patrick demanded, moving closer to Sandi and glaring at Dennis.

Jack silently applauded his son. He wasn't even going to say anything about that hint of whine in his voice.

Dennis suddenly remembered who would be paying his commission.

"I'm sorry, Mr. O'Connor,'' he apologized. "Sandi and I went to school together.''

"Yes, I gathered that," he murmured, gracious now that Dennis was no longer concentrating on Sandi. Now he was grateful she wore a longer skirt and didn't display her lovely legs.

Dennis ushered them out to his car as he described the first house he would be showing them.

"If you like traditional, you'll like this house. It's a lovely colonial style," he droned as he drove. "It's a two story with three bedrooms, two and a half baths, a solarium off the back of the house, pool and spa, barbecue pit and two cabanas near the pool. It's about a mile from the beach in a lovely neighborhood."

When they arrived, Jack barely looked at the front of the house and knew he didn't like it. Not wanting to dismiss something that could be doable, he didn't say anything as Dennis parked in the curved driveway.

Jack got out and looked at the immaculate lawn with its line of shrubbery that shielded the house from the street. The grass was so well kept, it looked as if it were made from green velvet. He held out his hand to Sandi, assisting her out of the seat.

She also looked around.

"Astroturf looks more real," she murmured. "Do you think they buy it by the yard? Pardon the pun."

He chuckled. "You probably aren't too far off."

"Can't you just visualize the gardener on his hands and knees using manicure scissors to keep the lawn at just the right height." She turned to follow Dennis up the steps.

They entered the house, where Jack took in priceless antiques, silk wallpaper and more rare glassware than he'd seen in a museum. He craned his head to stare upward at the highly polished stairway leading to the second floor.

"If this house had been antebellum, the stairs would have been perfect for Rhett Butler," Sandi muttered, keeping a close eye on Patrick, who, luckily, stuck close to her.

Jack easily plugged into the fantasy, then quickly tamped it down. The realtor guided them methodically through the house and outlying buildings. He was relieved that Patrick was so in awe of his surroundings that he stayed away from anything that looked breakable. The boy kept a hand tightly clasped in Sandi's, and he stayed close to her side.

They had just returned to the downstairs area, when a silver-haired woman wearing a beige silk dress walked through the front door.

"Dennis," she greeted the realtor with a faint smile. A smile that broadened as she noticed Jack. "You must be Mr. O'Connor. I'm Eleanor Bradley." She held out a well-manicured hand decorated with an ornate black-pearl-and-diamond ring.

"Mrs. Bradley." He shook her hand. "You have a lovely house here."

Her smile broadened at his compliment, then dimmed as she noticed Patrick and Sandi behind him. A hint of panic showed in her eyes before she could mask it.

"You don't have any kids, do you?" Patrick piped up.

She stared at him for a moment as if she hadn't expected him to speak. "No, young man, we do not."

He nodded as if he'd already guessed her answer. "I guess that's why you don't have any place for kids to play outside."

She smiled frostily. "Considering your father's future in the community, I would think he would be more concerned with a house for entertaining than setting up a childrens' play area.''

"Actually, Mrs. Bradley, I don't believe in doing a lot of business entertaining in my home," Jack coolly informed her. "That's what good restaurants are for. I prefer to keep my home and business life separated. Thank you for letting us look at your house. It's very lovely."

He looked sideways when they left and noticed that Mrs. Bradley immediately examined a vase Patrick had stood by.

"That wasn't a home unless you consider it a model home," Sandi muttered to Jack. "While all that silk wallpaper is lovely, it wouldn't last five minutes with kids running around. We won't even talk about what would happen to all that glassware. That woman would have a stroke if we had a fairly strong earthquake up this way."

"Dennis, is the second house anything like what we just saw?" Jack asked the realtor.

He looked startled. "Well, yes and no. Of course, the Bradley home is considered a showplace in the area. It's even been photographed for several home magazines. The other house I have in mind is just as large, but isn't as nice." He glanced at Patrick. "No collections of rare glass or silk wallpaper, if that relieves your mind."

"It does. What I want is a family home. A place Patrick can bring his friends if he desires. I don't care about a house that was photographed for magazines or a house for entertaining. I'm looking for a home. Not a house," he said pointedly.

Dennis drummed his fingers against the steering wheel as he searched his mind for possibilities. "Then let's discard the other house. I apologize. I guess I thought you were looking for a house that you could show off. Most people down here prefer that.''

"Not me," Jack said firmly.

"I want a big backyard for me and my dog," Patrick added. "And a swing and a slide and a treehouse." He thought for a moment. "I guess I need a tree, too. And near the beach!"

Dennis looked at Jack.

"Precisely," Jack said, nodding his agreement.

Dennis silently considered the possibilities. "There is one place," he said hesitantly. "More a family home."

Sandi glanced at Jack. "If you want neighbors like the Montgomerys and Spencers, then you should look around here. If you want neighbors who don't blink twice at kids running through a house at warp speed and lawns that don't look as if they're fake, you'll definitely have to look elsewhere."

"Let's look at the one you just mentioned," Jack told Dennis.

It didn't take long for him to see the difference in neighborhoods. Jack could see what she meant. The houses were older, some not as well cared for as they could be, but the area was clearly what he was looking for. He saw kids playing in yards and had an idea Patrick wouldn't waste any time asking for a bicycle.

He noticed Sandi looking out the window, seeming to take notes in her head.

"Dennis, is the Edwards's house still for sale?" Sandi asked suddenly.

"No one's wanted it yet, I guess, because of the price." He looked uneasy at his candor. "Um, yeah, it's still available."

She turned to Jack. "It might be just what you're looking for. It's a custom-built house set on the beach. I was down here for spring vacation when they were building it. It's only about three years old. The owner had it built to his specifications, then, due to a death in the family, never moved in. I've never been inside, but from what I've heard about the interior, it sounds like the kind of house you're looking for."

"It's always been kept up," Dennis explained, turning the wheel and driving down a side road. It wasn't long before he parked in front of a three-car garage and an attached building on the other side.

The moment Jack stepped out of the van and viewed the sprawling split-level house with its weathered cedar and brick front, he knew he'd found the house meant for him and Patrick. Keeping his features carefully schooled, he moved closer to study the front of the house. He glanced at the addition to the other side of the garage.

"That room was set up to be a home office for the owner," Dennis explained, gesturing to one side. "It has an outside entrance, but you can also go through the garage to reach the house. It's already been set up for multiline telephones." He unlocked the front door and waited for them to enter. "It's larger than it looks from the front, since it's actually two levels." He walked across the empty room to French doors and opened them wide. The tangy scent of sea air immediately engulfed them, chasing away the mustiness that accompanied an uninhabited house. He gestured toward winding stairs. "There are five bedrooms downstairs and a wraparound deck that gives you a great view of the water. This level consists of the kitchen, living room, dining room and a large family room."

Sandi walked around the room feeling a sense of awe coming over her. She wasn't sure why the sense of wonder flooded her soul. She couldn't remember ever feeling the way she did at that moment, but she understood the sensation rushing through her.

She felt as if she'd come home.

She felt the urge to see everything. She happily wandered through each room. She opened cabinets in the kitchen and studied their spacious interiors. She liked that. She took her time inspecting the built-in hutch in the dining room with tiny lights inside and admiring skylights that allowed natural light to flood into each room. She was so intent, she didn't notice Jack and Dennis had made their way to the downstairs portion of the house. As she looked around, she wondered if Jack felt the same connection to the house as she did. It was perfect for Patrick. Heck, it was perfect for her!

JACK SILENTLY BLESSED the other man for knowing when to keep his mouth shut as he inspected a house he already knew he was going to buy.

He had no doubt the house was solidly built, but no matter how much he liked the house, he'd want to see a structural-engineering report first. He admired the yard set off to the side instead of behind the house. It boasted a sturdy perimeter fence, as well as a wrought-iron fence with a locked gate circling the swimming pool and spa. He had no doubt Patrick would cast his vote for this house. He'd even bet that Sandi would give her seal of approval. She seemed to look pretty happy as she stuck her head inside cabinets and murmured good things about the walk-in pantry.

For a man who'd never intended to buy a home, he

felt as if this one was meant for him and Patrick. Along with the right woman.

He turned to Dennis.

"Why don't we go back to your office and discuss the house."

Dennis started to grin then quickly sobered.

"All right," he said casually.

Jack hid his own smile of satisfaction. There was nothing he liked better than wheeling and dealing. He was going to enjoy himself.

Patrick wasn't happy at being parted from the house he declared as absolutely perfect, but the idea that his dad was going to talk to the realtor about it today had him scrambling into the car.

"Even the grass is varying lengths," Sandi said cheerfully as she climbed into the car next to Patrick.

"I'll take Patrick across the street for some ice cream while you pulverize Dennis with your bargaining skills," Sandi said in a low voice after they returned to the realty office.

"What makes you so sure I'm going to pulverize him?" he asked, amused by her statement.

"Because, it's obvious you love the wheeling and dealing part of business. You already look as if you're eager to get into the game. You enjoy getting the upper hand and keeping it there. Poor Dennis doesn't have a chance." She wrinkled her nose. "Which is why I'm taking Patrick away from here. I don't want him picking up any of your bad habits. Patrick?" She grasped the boy's hand and headed for the door. "C'mon, sweetie, we're going for ice cream while your father plays businessman."

He hopped along beside her. "Cool!"

Jack stayed at the window, watching them cross the

street. Sandi's head was bent slightly as Patrick chattered away. He remained there until they disappeared inside the sweet shop.

"Sandi always loved kids," Dennis said. "I'm surprised she hasn't had a houseful by now."

"I guess she hasn't had much time for a social life, what with her dedication to her teaching and all," he commented, not sure he liked discussing Sandi with another man. Still... Dennis had grown up with her and it seemed the two of them knew each other pretty well.

"I heard she was living with some guy up in Seattle. I thought her sister said they were going to get married." Dennis sat at his desk and rummaged through the drawers.

Jack suddenly felt cold inside. "Really?"

He hoped if he kept his expression noncommittal he might learn more about this man Sandi was supposed to marry and whether or not he truly was out of the picture or would be reappearing at the end of the summer. Sandi hadn't mentioned having a man in her life, and it wasn't a question he would have asked her. He walked over to the desk and took the chair across from Dennis.

Dennis nodded. He finally found the papers he was looking for and pulled them out. "Her sister said she was positive Sandi would get married before she did. I guess it didn't work out." He pulled a blank piece of paper in front of him and began writing. When he finished, he pushed it across the desk toward Jack. "This is the seller's asking price."

Jack didn't bother picking up the paper. He could see all he wanted to. His smile resembled that of a wolf spotting its prey.

"All right. Now we can talk about my counteroffer."

"DO YOU THINK I COULD SLEEP outside when we move there?" Patrick asked as he dipped his spoon into his marshmallow sundae. He swirled the sticky cream into the chocolate ice cream, then around his spoon before he stuck it into his mouth. "With a sleeping bag and everything? My dog could protect me, ya know."

"Are you sure you want to sleep outside when you could have that big room all to yourself? Of course, your dog wouldn't be allowed in there. Not with all the mirrors on the walls. He might accidentally run into them and break them," Sandi said with a wicked gleam in her eye. "I'm sure Mrs. Bradley will take all her vases with her, so you won't have to worry about breaking any of them. Until your dad gets vases of his own, that is."

Patrick stuck his finger down his throat and made rude gagging noises.

"Dad won't buy that yucky house," he confidently stated. "It was too ugly. 'Sides, that lady didn't like kids. She looked at me like I had mud on my shoes. I bet she wouldn't want Dad to buy her old house."

Sandi silently agreed with her young charge. She hadn't missed how Mrs. Bradley had looked at Patrick as if he'd suddenly beamed down from another galaxy and brought the creeping crud with him. She was positive the older woman would burn the house down first.

"Some people consider their house a showplace," she explained.

"What's that?"

"It's like when you put out your important toys for other kids to see, but not to play with."

"Except I do let other kids play with my toys," he admitted.

Sandi grinned and ruffled his hair with her hand.

Patrick swirled more of his treat around his spoon. "Dad will buy the house that's by the beach so I can go swimming all the time. And it has a really big yard for a dog and maybe a cat. Do cats and dogs like hamsters?" he asked.

"It depends on the dog and cat, but sometimes they don't like smaller animals," she replied, tipping the small cup of hot fudge onto her vanilla ice cream then adding a spoonful of peanuts to the concoction. She loved the option of building her own sundae. There were times when hot fudge was a necessity. Today was one of those days. Patrick kept his sundae simple with marshmallow crème and chocolate ice cream, although Sandi did talk him into topping it with cut-up M&M's. She realized her mistake when he practically covered the ice cream with the candies.

"You mean they'd hurt it?" He looked concerned.

"Not hurt it exactly," she said carefully. "But a cat might look at a hamster and think it's a mouse."

"And he'd chase it like Tom chases Jerry?"

Sandi nodded. "That's why you keep a hamster in a cage where he can be safe, and you only bring him out to play when the other animals are outside. And you make sure he can't go anywhere where he could get hurt."

She hoped she wasn't giving Patrick more ideas to add to his zoo. Come to think of it, she hadn't recalled his mentioning a hamster before. Oops. Jack was *not* going to be happy about this!

"I want you to think about something very carefully, Patrick. If you have too many pets, you can't give them the attention they need. If you stay inside too much playing with your hamster, your dog will feel sad because you're not outside playing with him. The same if you have a cat. Is that fair to your dog or cat?" She then remained silent to allow Patrick to think about what she'd said. She always tried to make her points as simple as possible then give the kids a chance to consider what she said and make a decision on their own.

He slurped the rapidly melting ice cream from his spoon. He grinned sheepishly when Sandi shot him a look meant to chastise. "I'd rather have a dog, cuz he could go down to the beach with me. I don't think hamsters could swim very good. And cats really hate water." He ate a couple more bites. "Fish would be okay, wouldn't they? You can't play with them, but you can look at them."

She laughed. "You still need to talk to your dad about any pets you have in mind."

"Oh, I'll talk to him." He displayed the same confidence his father demonstrated.

"What do you plan to talk to me about?" Jack slid into the chair beside Sandi. He eyed her sundae then cast her a look of disbelief.

"What?" She sounded more than a little defensive as she poured another healthy dollop of hot fudge on her ice cream.

"Nothing." He backed off, as well he should. "What's good here?" He picked up the menu printed in calligraphy and pretended interest in the contents.

"Anything with chocolate in it," Sandi replied. She gestured toward one wall that held a variety of dishes and containers. "If you're adventurous, go for the all-you-can-eat, build-your-own-sundae bar. Then you can do anything you want with it. Consider it a salad bar but with ice cream."

Jack gave the teenage waitress his order and listened to her instructions on how to build his own sundae. He left for the rear of the shop and began filling his dish.

"He bought the house," Patrick said confidently. He dug into his ice cream with renewed relish.

"Listen to you! What? Do you think he bought it just because you want it?" she teased.

He nodded. "You'll see." He impatiently waited until his father sat down. "You bought the house, didn't you? The really neat house." He looked expectant.

Jack appeared surprised. "Was I supposed to buy that house? Are you sure you weren't hoping I'd buy the first house we looked at?"

"Yep." There was no doubt in Patrick's mind his father would do the right thing.

Jack didn't answer. Instead, he dug his spoon into scoops of chocolate and vanilla ice cream sprinkled with crushed chocolate mints, Oreos and chocolate chip cookie dough.

Sandi eyed his concoction with amazement. "I am impressed. You built a grade-A sundae and, believe me, I know about grade-A sundaes."

He took several bites, nodding his head in satisfaction. "No reason not to do something right when you've got the chance."

"Is the house ours?" Patrick persisted, more than a little impatient by now.

"We'll know by the end of the day. I heard the

selling price, I counteroffered, the owner countered my counteroffer and, after I made my final offer, he asked for some time to think it over.''

"Considering how long it's stood empty, I bet he'll take it," Sandi said. "I suggest you either have him pay for a cleaning crew or hire one first thing. There's more than just plain old-fashioned dust in that house." When he shot her a teasing look, she quickly added, "Don't even think about it. I'm a nanny, not a maid, I consider dust bunnies my best friends and not the least bit dangerous."

"I could ask, couldn't I?" he asked innocently, scooping up ice cream and topping and sliding the spoon into his mouth.

"Steffi got the clean freak gene. I got the if-you-can't-write-your-name-on-the-furniture-it's-not-time-to-dust gene," she told him.

"Can you really write your name on furniture?" Patrick asked, wide-eyed.

Sandi grinned. "It's not really a good idea, Patrick, even if it sounds like fun. That's why we practice our writing on the sand, where it's a much better game because we can use seashells and sticks. You can't use them on furniture, can you?"

He took a moment to think about it, as if the idea was intriguing. Then he caught his father's gaze and sheepishly shook his head.

Jack's cellular phone rang and he quickly pulled it out. He turned away and spoke quietly into the receiver. A few moments later, he disconnected the call and turned around. He looked cheerful when he glanced at his son.

"You wanted that race-car bed for your new bedroom, didn't you?"

Patrick's eyes grew saucer wide. "A new bedroom?" he whispered. "We're gonna have a house?"

Jack nodded. "And you'll have your race-car bed, if you still want it."

The boy's head bobbed so much his hair fell forward on his forehead. "And a puppy."

"Let's work on getting moved in and finding furniture before we talk about adding a dog to the insanity," he told him.

Sandi silently agreed, as they made their way out of the ice-cream parlor and jubilantly headed back to the hotel.

Once inside their suite, Jack went over to the desk and opened his DayRunner.

"You suggested I bring in a cleaning crew. Do you know of anyone good?" he asked, starting to jot down notes.

"I'm sure Dennis can give you names. Or I can ask Steffi. I haven't been back here all that much for the past few years," she replied. "Otherwise, I'm sure Mrs. Montgomery can give you names of the right crews to use." She grinned to take any sting out of her words. "I bet she'd even offer to supervise them."

"Snob," he teased back. "Would you ask your sister please?" He didn't want to call Grace if he could help it. He feared that if he did, he'd suddenly end up with a housekeeper, cook, chauffeur and God knows what else. She'd probably even tell him he would have been better off taking the Bradley house. He shuddered at that thought. He wanted a home, not a showplace. Maybe Patrick had the right idea, after all. A place where a mom could bake cookies and smell good. He lifted his eyes to gaze at Sandi.

She admitted she could bake cookies. She most definitely smelled good. Looked even better. There was no doubt how much she loved children. Patrick told him she read great bedtime stories. The latter brought a lot of interesting notions to mind.

Except, when it came to the idea of bedtime activities, Jack had something entirely different in mind.

Chapter Six

"I like this one best." Patrick announced. He started to swipe his mouth clean with the back of his hand, then caught Sandi's silent warning. He grinned and accepted the paper napkin she held out to him. "Thank you."

She nodded her silent approval at his remembering his manners. "You said you liked the last one best."

"I did. Then you gave me this one." He looked over the offerings with cheerful expectancy. "What's next?"

"He's doing better at this than we are," Steffi said. "I'm almost feeling queasy," she softly confided, leaning back in her chair. "I never thought I'd ever say I never want to look at another piece of cake in my lifetime."

"Welcome to the club." Sandi couldn't look at the various samples of wedding cake still displayed on a glass platter.

Different flavors of cake and fillings along with buttercream and whipped frosting had been set out for them to try. For the past hour, they had nibbled and discarded a few and set aside others for the final choosing.

By now, Patrick was the only one still enthusiastic about the task. Both women started taking smaller bites and drinking more water.

"Why not chocolate?" he asked.

"There's chocolate rum, but it seemed kind of heavy," Steffi replied. "Chocolate is really more for birthday parties than weddings."

"I'll have a chocolate wedding cake," he declared.

"I wouldn't worry about planning your wedding cake just yet," Sandi teased. "And don't forget your bride-to-be will have some say in what kind of cake you'll have."

"What are you doing, Sandi? Marrying your young charge off already?"

Sandi looked up and smiled at the man entering the bakery.

"Karl!" She hopped up and ran over to hug him. "We're helping Steffi sample cakes."

He walked over to the table and examined the remains.

"Want to try one?" Steffi asked, pushing the platter in his direction.

Karl chuckled. "I came in for one of Magda's macaroons to go with my afternoon coffee. That is all I dare have if I don't want to have to alter my own clothing."

"I didn't know you could eat lots of cake and then pick one," Patrick said excitedly. "This is a lot of fun."

Karl glanced at Sandi. "And what do you call the lesson you are giving young Patrick today?"

"Snack time," she said promptly. She started to pick up another cake square, then put it back down. "Stef, I don't think I can eat another bite."

Steffi grimaced as she looked at the rejected cake. "I don't think I can, either."

"I'll finish them." Patrick started to reach for the platter, but Sandi swept it from him.

"No, that's okay. I vote for the raspberry filling," Sandi told her sister.

Karl inspected the cake squares, chose the appropriate one and picked it up. He bit off a corner and slowly chewed.

"The raspberry would do very nicely," he agreed.

Steffi looked undecided. "Still, the custard was very good."

"But your colors are a dark pink—that's almost a raspberry color—and a paler pink for accent. The raspberry would go perfectly with your colors," Sandi pointed out. She wasn't sure, but she suspected she was flying on a sugar high. "Please don't make us try them again."

"I'm willing!" Patrick piped up.

She doubted this was what Jack had expected her to do with his son when she'd explained they would be helping Steffi with wedding preparations today. Over Patrick's protests, Jack told her he could keep Patrick that afternoon for her. She had assured him that they needed Patrick's help.

She knew if Patrick was hyper for the rest of the day, it would be up to her to bring him back down to earth.

"Raspberry it is," Steffi decided, pushing her chair back and getting up. "There is no way I can eat any more."

"Can we take home what's left?" Patrick asked hopefully.

Sandi groaned.

"Come, Patrick, help me choose a nice macaroon to go with my coffee," Karl invited.

Patrick hopped up and went with him.

"Do you enjoy the time you spend with Sandi?" Karl asked once they reached the glass display cases and were out of earshot of the two sisters.

Patrick eyed a tray filled with frosted cookies.

"Yeah. She takes me to the park, and we do lots of neat things there. I met some kids that might be in kindergarten with me," he replied. "She took me to the beach and showed me tide pools, where we saw all kinds of tiny fish and weird looking flowers. I told her I want her to be my teacher when I start kindergarten."

"So you like her."

Patrick nodded. He looked over his shoulder and, once assured Sandi couldn't eavesdrop, he leaned toward the older man.

"I like her a lot," he confided. "I think it would be really neat if Sandi became my mom. Do you think she would want to be my mom? I know Dad likes her, too."

Karl placed his hand on top of Patrick's head. "Yes, I think she would like to be your mother very much."

The boy's face lit up. "Think I should ask her?"

Karl shook his head. "Not just yet. Sometimes grown-ups realize on their own what's in store for them. But if they need help, we will help them, yes?"

Patrick's head bobbed up and down. "Yes," he added for emphasis.

JACK DIDN'T LIKE LYING awake half the night.

He was used to climbing into bed and falling asleep by the time his head hit his pillow. With a good night's sleep, he could get up in the morning and deal with his clients with a clear head and a sharp mind.

It was easy to see that tonight wasn't going to be one of those nights.

If he wasn't mistaken, the last time he had a good night's sleep was before he hired a nanny.

Funny, when he thought of nannies, he thought of Mary Poppins. Or plain-looking women who wore shapeless uniforms and silently blended with the walls while they efficiently guided and instructed their tiny charges.

They weren't supposed to have hair that gleamed like a precious metal in the sunshine or laughter that rivaled the musical wind chimes that hung on the hotel balconies. While her manner of dress wasn't deliberately provocative, there was no way she would blend into any background. He should call himself crazy for just wanting to check out what color polish she used on her toenails.

She'd captivated Patrick the way the Piped Piper had ensnared the rats, and Jack felt as if he was, likewise, powerless against her siren song.

He rolled over and punched his pillow into shape.

Patrick had marched into the suite carrying a container. He handed it to his father, explaining it was filled with cake samples. When Jack asked Sandi if she wanted any, she looked a little green and let him know she'd had more than her share of wedding cake, thank you very much.

Jack wondered how many boys got to spend an afternoon helping choose a wedding cake.

Only with Sandi was such an afternoon possible.

Only with Sandi.

He was thinking more and more of what he'd like

to do only with Sandi. He could blame it on not being with a woman for some time. But he'd be telling himself a whopper of a lie.

He was just starting to drift off when he heard a muffled sound from the parlor. He identified it as the sliding door opening.

Deciding he should check it out, Jack pulled on a pair of shorts and left his room. When he reached the open sliding door, he found Sandi seated on a chair with the small table in front of her. Her bare feet were propped on the edge of the table, and she was leaning over her bent knees, which were covered by a mint-colored gauzy fabric.

"Couldn't sleep?" he said softly.

She looked up and over her shoulder. One hand held a small brush hovering over her toes.

"I like coming out here late at night when all you hear is the ocean," she replied, using her brush to gesture to the other chair. "How about you?"

Jack walked over and settled in the chair with his legs stretched out in front of him. He noted the nail polish bottle held a shimmery navy shade.

"I started thinking about my kindergarten teacher," he said suddenly.

She looked intrigued. She bent over and carefully applied polish to the toes on her left foot. "Good memories?"

"Mrs. Benton. To me, she was old as dirt, although she was probably in her fifties. She always smelled like chalk, and sometimes her teeth clicked when she talked. But she dug right in the fingerpaints with us." He smiled and shook his head as memories swept over him. "But she never painted her toes wild colors, and she never took us to a bakery where we would sample different wedding cakes. In fact, she always lectured us that sweets were bad for us. Of course, that never stopped us from wanting cupcakes in our lunches.''

"Mine was Miss Turner," Sandi said. "She was definitely old as dirt in my eyes, because she was in her sixties. She wore support hose, took a nap during our rest time and could never tell Steffi and me apart. I don't think she ever tried. She told our mother that she was convinced we would come to no good."

"And you became a kindergarten teacher even after all that?" he asked.

She nodded. "And now my students are convinced I'm as old as dirt and hate it that I insist they behave when they'd rather get into mischief. If I'm lucky, one student will remember me a little fondly."

Jack studied the expanse of bare leg and hint of thigh left visible by the bunched up fabric. There was no way he could think of her as a teacher. Not with those legs. "I'd say your male students will remember you more than a little fondly. I know I would."

Sandi's eyes were uptilted just slightly with a smile that left him breathless.

"Why, Mr. O'Connor, sir, if I didn't know any better, I would think you were flirting with me," she drawled, sounding like a demure belle of the Old South.

"I never considered it a crime to let a woman know she was attractive." He could blame it on the late-night hour or the air or whatever later on. For now, he decided to relax and enjoy the moment.

Sandi went back to painting her toenails with careful even strokes. Once finished, she stretched her legs out and eyed her work.

"Why the wild colors?" Jack asked.

She tipped her head from one side to the other as she gazed at her feet.

"The first school I worked for was very conservative. Not only did the kids have to wear specific uniforms, but the teachers were under a strict dress code, too. Black or navy skirt one inch before the knee, white or cream colored blouse, nothing sheer or sleeveless, plain pumps, no open toes. Very minimal makeup and no nail polish."

"And since your toes were hidden by your shoes, you decided that's how you would rebel," he guessed.

She grinned. "I wore the brightest red nail polish I could find and absolutely wicked lingerie."

Jack was positive the air around him suddenly heated up a good fifty degrees. Visions of Sandi wearing red lingerie and red nail polish danced through his head. He licked lips that were suddenly dry and coughed to clear his throat.

She tentatively touched her nails with a fingertip. Assured they were dry enough, she turned her chair around so she could face him.

"Did I shock you?"

"Did you want to?"

She shrugged. "Maybe a little. Steffi's the quiet one who ate all her peas. I was the one who snuck my peas under the table to the dog. For Show and Tell one time, I took in a copy of Dad's *Playboy*. My teacher had me write a five-hundred-word essay on why you shouldn't take your parents' things without permission, and my parents grounded me for a month."

"How did your teachers handle having twins in the classroom?" He was intrigued with the way the breeze billowed her gown around her ankles. He could even swear he caught hints of her perfume in the air.

Sandi shook her head. "After kindergarten, our parents insisted we always be in different classes. We were twins, but we didn't dress alike, and even our hairstyles weren't alike. They wanted people to see us as individuals."

"How did you feel about it?" he asked. "I would think most twins would like the attention."

"It didn't stop us from exchanging clothes and pretending to be each other. It was too much fun. But we were also able to have our own identity. Steffi took ballet. I took gymnastics. I was a cheerleader in high school and she was on the track team. We had our own interests and followed them."

"And you grew up to be a kindergarten teacher and she started her own catering business," Jack commented.

Sandi nodded. "Steffi always loved to plan events and she's good at it. She used to plan our birthday parties around themes. One year it was a circus, another it was an old-fashioned tea party. When we gave our parents a surprise twenty-fifth anniversary party, Steffi gathered up old record albums that were released the year they got married, she recreated the menu from their wedding reception and took their wedding photographs and had them blown up to poster size. All the music played and the clothing the guests wore was from that year. When you entered the ballroom it was like returning to the sixties." Her face was soft and alight with memories. She suddenly giggled. "Some of the women shouldn't have worn minis, but it was a lot of fun to remember that time period."

"It sounds as if you gave them something very special."

"We did," she whispered. She straightened up. "And I guess I'll be doing the same for Steffi in twenty-five years for her anniversary."

"What about you?" Jack asked, curious about any men that might have been in her life. "No men ready to sweep you off your feet?"

"Not for a while." She stood up and stretched her arms over her head.

As he looked at her in her gauzy nightgown and hair blowing in the night breeze, he thought of how easy it would be to seduce her. There was no doubt she was attracted to him. And he couldn't help but be attracted to her. She was so much like a free spirit.

He stood up and slowly reached out for her. It took little urging for Sandi to step closer to him and lift her face to his.

She tasted like the night around them. Enticing and addictive.

Jack knew there were many men who would take advantage of the moment. It would be easy to do when the atmosphere was this romantic, and they were both clearly in the mood. But he wasn't one of those men. Especially not with his son asleep only a matter of yards away.

When his hands dropped from her shoulders, she stepped away. Her eyes were wide as she looked up at him.

"Good night, Jack," she murmured, circling around him and heading for the parlor.

He stood there for some time, listening to the quiet *snick* of her bedroom door closing.

"There's something to be said for a nice cold shower before bed," he told himself.

SANDI NEVER GAVE JACK any indication the kiss they'd shared on the balcony remained in her memory. He was grateful she wasn't uneasy around him. He'd stolen the kiss and didn't regret it. He was just biding his time until it was right for another.

After breakfast, Sandi had borne Patrick off with the breezy explanation that they were having a very special math lesson.

Jack had agreed to meet a prospective client for breakfast, and after they finished their business, he utilized the hotel's fitness center for a nice long run on the treadmill. He figured if he tired himself out enough, he wouldn't think of Sandi quite so much.

When he returned to his suite, he found a message from Karl asking him if he was available for lunch. Jack immediately returned his call and arranged to meet him at the plaza café a few doors down from Karl's shop.

By the time he reached the outdoor café, Karl was already seated under a blue-and-white striped umbrella. Most of the tables were already filled with other diners enjoying the early afternoon sun.

"One of my clients told me about available office space at the Hillside Office Complex, and I thought you might be interested," Karl began after Jack had ordered a glass of wine from the waitress. "The leasing agent is the same one who handles this plaza. The man is excellent at keeping the tenants happy and maintenance up-to-date." He handed Jack a business card. "The offices over there are strictly business and financial, which should be perfect for you."

"I'll look into it, thank you." He tucked the card into his shirt pocket. "How is it going for you?"

"Weddings are always popular this time of year," the older man replied, adding a bit more sugar to his coffee and stirring it. "I only hope J.T. makes it back in time for his final tuxedo fitting. The man seems to think if he sends me his measurements, I can assure his clothing will fit him perfectly." He shook his head in frustration over Jack's friend, who firmly believed in living by his own rules.

"To be honest, I'd be surprised if he showed up for Whitney and Dylan's wedding," Jack commented, smiling at the waitress as she deposited a glass of wine in front of him. "At the rate he was going, he wasn't going to make it for Cori and Dylan's wedding. I have no idea what's going on with him anymore."

"I have an idea a great deal is going on in his mind. Things that he needs to take care of. He has to realize he will have to return here if he intends to resolve some very old issues," Karl said, consulting the menu and finally making his decision.

Jack frowned. "Old issues? What old issues could J.T. have here?"

Karl waved his hand as if plucking answers out of the air. "Everyone has old issues. Yours are with Patrick's grandmother."

He sipped his wine even as he wished it was something stronger. "Harriet and I are fine."

The older man smiled. "Do not lie to an old man, Jack. Especially one who sees as much as I do. Just remember she is not your enemy and all will be fine."

Jack chuckled. "Are you sure you weren't Confucius in another life?"

Karl straightened up. "No matter what life I have

lived, I was always a Russian," he stated in a regal tone. "And I will add that Rasputin was not one of my former lives."

Jack laughed and the two men began eating the salads the waitress had left them. After the men ordered their meal, Karl smiled at Jack.

"And how is young Patrick enjoying having Sandi as his nanny?"

"Very much," he replied. "She seems to turn much of their playtime into a teaching session. They're having a math lesson today."

Karl started chuckling and appeared not able to stop. Jack looked puzzled as he tried to figure out why the man was so amused.

"After we eat, I suggest you stop by the Galloway Catering office. It's in this plaza, across from the florist, so you can't miss it. There you will see how his math lesson is accomplished in a most interesting way. Now, tell me what you have been doing since the reception."

Jack immediately began telling Karl about the house he bought and how happy Patrick was to have a backyard. Karl nodded, commenting about how he knew the house well and how he was certain they would be happy there. He offered a few suggestions for services Jack would require, and the men pleasantly passed the next hour as they enjoyed their food.

It didn't stop Jack from wondering what Karl alluded to about Sandi and Patrick. Obviously he knew something Jack didn't, and he found it highly amusing.

He was ready to excuse himself to find out for himself, when a woman's voice cut in.

"What a shame there isn't a gentlemen's club

nearby for the two of you to hide out in where you can have your brandy and cigars.''

Jack looked up, prepared to smile and greet Grace Montgomery. His smile dipped a little when he noticed her companion. ''Good afternoon, Harriet.''

''Jack.'' She looked beyond him. ''Isn't Patrick with you?''

''He's with Sandi.''

Grace offered a thin smile. ''Yes, you did say you'd hired her.'' She sounded as if she'd hoped Jack might have changed his mind and hired a more suitable applicant.

Karl stood up. ''Ladies, please grace our table with your lovely presence.'' He pulled out the chair next to him, which Grace accepted, while Jack assisted Harriet into the remaining chair.

''Have you eaten?'' Karl asked.

They explained they'd lunched with friends before stopping by the plaza to meet with the florist for the upcoming wedding.

''Did you find your nanny through an agency, Jack?'' Harriet asked.

''No,'' he said promptly, feeling a bit uneasy under Harriet's gaze, even if it only revealed curiosity. ''Miss Galloway was referred to me. Even if she's never worked as a nanny before, she's fully qualified to look after Patrick. During the school year, she works as a kindergarten teacher.''

Grace took up where he left off. ''Sandra Galloway recently moved back to Montgomery Beach to help her sister with her wedding. Her sister was our caterer. I didn't think Sandra would give up teaching.''

''She hasn't,'' he replied, not wanting to go into any more detail.

"But who will look after Patrick in the fall when she returns to teaching?" Harriet asked.

Jack looked at Karl, hoping the older man would have the right answer, but he had turned away to say something to Grace in a low tone. Jack turned back to Harriet and opened his mouth in hopes he would say the right thing, when he was rescued by a small whirlwind descending on him.

"It was so cool, Dad!" Patrick climbed up onto his father's lap. Sandi followed more slowly. "I counted forty thousand napkins."

"Not even close, pardner," Sandi corrected him.

Patrick looked across the table and brightened up when he saw Harriet. "Grandma! Sandi taught me how to count really, really high," he proudly announced. "I still musta counted more than a thousand napkins."

"That's wonderful, dear. Oh!" She laughed when he launched himself into her lap. He looped his arms around her neck and smacked a noisy kiss on her cheek. "What else did Sandi teach you?"

Jack could have sworn a bit of light went out of Sandi's eyes as she smiled at the group.

"If you don't mind, I'll return to my sister's office and pick up some things I need," she murmured.

"Go ahead, Sandi, I'll keep Patrick here," Jack told her.

"And Steffi asked me if I want to be her ring bearer when she gets married!" Patrick chattered, practically bouncing with his excitement. "I can, can't I? That way I can wear my tuxedo again! I need to wear it more before I grow too big and it doesn't fit me anymore."

"Sure, you can be her ring bearer," he told him.

"You can think of it as practice for Whitney and Dylan's wedding."

"Tell Steffi I can do it!" Patrick shouted after Sandi.

The two women winced at his exuberant voice.

"Dear, are you sure she's proper for Patrick?" Grace asked Jack, a frown marring her forehead as she watched Sandi walk away. "She may have the training as a teacher, but a nanny does so much more than a teacher does. And has a great deal more responsibility, since she's with the child twenty-four hours a day. She also usually wears something more appropriate," she murmured, not missing Sandi's khaki shorts that bared a great deal of leg and tangerine cotton halter top that bared her tanned shoulders and midriff.

"She does have the necessary references, doesn't she?" Harriet asked over the top of Patrick's head. "After all, you are an important man in your own right. Not to mention a wealthy one. Some of the stories nowadays of what can happen..." She lightly shuddered. "I know you would do everything possible to protect him."

Jack was tempted to tell the women that speaking over Patrick didn't mean he didn't hear what they were saying. He picked up his coffee cup and drank so he wouldn't say what he truly wanted to.

"Daddy bought a house and after we move in, I get to have a puppy," Patrick announced. "And I get to have a bed that looks like a race car."

The two women exchanged glances. Jack hated the silent conversation going between them.

"And will Miss Galloway live in?" Grace asked casually.

"Nannies usually do," Jack said tightly, holding on to his coffee cup.

"You have nothing to worry about with Sandi." Karl stepped into the breach. "I have seen her with Patrick, and they get along beautifully."

"Karl, you are a dear." Grace patted his hand. "But men never see this the way we women do. The woman we hire to take care of our children is very important. She must have impeccable references and have the right amount of training. She mustn't stand out and create a bad impression. That's so very important in our circle."

Jack's face tightened until his features appeared to be carved in stone. The last thing he wanted to do was create a scene in front of Patrick, but he didn't like what he was hearing. Who he hired was none of their business!

"Boys need the right guiding hand," Harriet chimed in.

"What any child needs is a parent around twenty-four hours a day," he said in clipped tones, unable to keep it reined in any longer. He stared coldly at both women. "He has me for that. Sandi provides another form of comfort, which he also needs. Kids need a parent foremost," he repeated, knowing full well Michelle had spent little time at her home while growing up. He wondered how he had missed that selfish side of her while they were together. Had he been so infatuated he hadn't seen what kind of woman she truly was?

Patrick looked from one adult face to the other. The tension seemed to radiate from one to the other like a smothering fog that even his young mind could comprehend. He wasn't entirely sure what was going on, but he sensed it had something to do with his beloved Sandi.

"It's okay, Grandma," he hurriedly assured Harriet. "Sandi can live with us, cuz she and Daddy are getting married."

Jack fervently wished he hadn't been drinking coffee at the time of Patrick's announcement. Then he wouldn't have choked and spat the liquid in a spray going in all directions.

Chapter Seven

There was no escaping the tiny brown droplets that spattered across Grace's white silk blouse and Karl's snowy white shirtfront.

"Oh, Daddy!" Patrick breathed, awed by this display of his father's new talent. "You spit coffee out your nose. Can you teach me to do that?"

Karl merely smiled as he dipped a corner of his napkin into his water glass and dabbed at the spots on his shirt. Grace looked horrified, and Harriet looked stunned by the bald announcement.

"It will come out easily," Karl told Jack, who sat there stunned by what he'd done.

"I'm sure Patrick was having a bit of fun with us," Grace said stiffly, ready to place blame where she felt it was due. "Making up stories seems to go along with little boys."

Karl shot her a look of gentle chastisement. "Patrick always speaks the truth, Grace," he said quietly. The woman's face turned a pale pink under his censure.

"They hardly know each other," she murmured.

Jack wasn't sure whether to haul his son away for a very stern talking to, give him the spanking he'd never had, or somehow save him from his whopper of a lie. For a moment, all three sounded good to him. There was just the question of which one to do first.

When he turned to his son, he couldn't miss the pleading in Patrick's eyes. The boy knew he'd done wrong, but he didn't want to be punished in front of the others. Not that Jack would even think of doing that, but what could he say to defuse the situation before it grew even more out of hand?

"Whoops. Did we have a food fight and I wasn't invited?" Sandi asked, as she walked up and stared at the coffee-spattered tablecloth. She narrowed her eyes at Patrick. "Can't trust you, can I?" she teased.

Patrick turned to Sandi with a cry of relief. "Sandi, it was so cool! Daddy spit coffee out his nose," he announced, running toward her, arms outstretched. "I asked him to teach me, but he said no."

"Umph!" She laughed as she just barely caught him. "Believe me, that's not one of the skills necessary for kindergarten, kiddo. We'll find something more fun for you to learn, okay? I'm sure you'll think of much worse things to do by the time you reach high school."

"Such as counting napkins?" Harriet asked. When Sandi turned to her, Harriet held out her hand. "I'm Harriet Anderson, Patrick's grandmother. I understand congratulations are in order for you and Jack."

Sandi released Patrick so she could take the woman's hand.

"Thank you," she said faintly, looking as if she knew exactly what the older woman was talking about. "As for counting napkins, it's more fun to learn counting if they have something tangible to count. And it was something different than counting blocks or sticks.''

''Is that how you teach your students to count?'' Grace asked. ''Using napkins?'' Her tone indicated she didn't feel it was an idea the board of education would approve of.

''We counted rocks one time. Another time we made tiny balls out of modeling clay and counted those according to color.'' Sandi glanced at Jack as if looking for an answer there. None was forthcoming. She felt like Alice did when she stumbled onto the Tea Party.

Harriet turned to Grace. ''We really should be going,'' she said. She stood up, smiling at the men and Sandi. ''I'm glad to have met you, Sandi,'' she told her. ''I'm sure I'll see you again.''

She and Grace started to gather up their bags, but Karl forestalled them and offered to carry their packages to the car. He said his goodbyes and followed the two women.

Sandi dropped into the chair Harriet had vacated. ''I couldn't have been gone for more than five minutes. And I come back to congratulations. What did I do?''

Patrick slid into a chair and hunkered down. He obviously knew he was in big trouble. ''I didn't want her saying bad things about Sandi,'' he muttered.

She stared at Jack. He heaved a deep sigh.

''Since the ladies didn't seem to like the idea of our sharing a house, Patrick decided to tell them it was all right since we were getting married.''

A tiny whimper started in the back of Sandi's throat and moved its way upward. She looked wildly around for a waiter and flagged one down.

"I'd like a glass of Chardonnay, please," she said in a husky whisper. "A very large glass."

"I DIDN'T WANT GRANDMA and Mrs. Montgomery saying Sandi was bad!" Patrick said in his defense as they later entered the hotel suite.

Jack thrust his fingers through his hair, then pressed the digits against his scalp as if the pain would take away the headache pounding across his temples. He closed his eyes.

"You lied, Patrick," he said sternly. "You know lies are bad."

The boy's lower lip stuck out, wobbling dangerously.

"I want you to go to your room and think about what you've done," Jack ordered grimly. "I'll be in later to talk to you."

"But, Dad!" he wailed.

Jack shook his head. "No 'but Dad.' Just turn yourself around and go to your room." He stared at his son. *"Now."*

Patrick's head was hanging as he shuffled his way to his room. Muffled whimpers could be heard as he walked away. When he entered his bedroom, he carefully closed the door behind him.

"He went in there as if he's entering a prison cell and he's going to be flogged at dawn," Sandi said, dropping into a nearby chair with the air of one who was completely exhausted.

"He should be so lucky," Jack muttered, pouring himself a glass of scotch and downing it quickly. He refilled the glass, but sipped the contents slowly this time. He dropped onto a stool and collapsed against the bar.

"I'm sure there are people who find humor in this kind of situation," he said. His fingers tapped the counter in a nervous cadence.

"So I guess this means Steffi doesn't have to dig out our grandfather's shotgun," Sandi quipped. She grimaced when Jack shot her a dark look that spoke volumes. "As you said, there are some people who find humor in this kind of situation. Obviously you're not one of them."

"And obviously you are one of them," he growled.

"Patrick felt he had a good reason for saying what he did."

"No matter the reason, he still lied. He knows how I feel about lying."

Sandi appeared to study her nails as she spoke. "Why do you think he needed to say what he did?"

Jack turned on the stool. One arm rested on the bar, his fingers curved around the squat glass still partially filled with amber liquid. His dark hair was tousled from the wind, but his expression held none of the relaxation his hair displayed. His once immaculate white shirt was dotted with brown spots she knew to be coffee. Even his dark eyes were so cold his stare should have turned her into a block of ice.

"He thought he was protecting your reputation."

She arched an eyebrow at his words. "And what would make him think my virtue needed protection?"

Jack's tanned features turned a dusky red. He lifted his glass and sipped.

"How do we know it wasn't you he was protecting?" she said softly. "I could see how uneasy you were around Mrs. Anderson. She doesn't look as if she'd step on a bug, but you acted as if she was going to walk all over you without a second thought. Why is that?"

"I was not uneasy around her," he argued.

"Were, too."

"Was not," he muttered, not realizing he'd fallen back into a speech pattern from his childhood.

But Sandi noticed and couldn't help grinning, a grin that barely took shape before dying.

How could she think of making jokes now when a few words had blown the world up around them.

She silently agreed that Patrick did wrong in lying to everyone. A part of her applauded his thinking up such a whopper in his attempt to protect her. Another part couldn't help but worry if this would be the end of her job. It would be only too easy to blame her for what happened.

She and Patrick had had such a fun day. He saw the catering shop as a colorful playground. When she'd set him to counting the varicolored napkins, she hadn't thought of it as work, but a way to make counting interesting. He'd been so proud to announce the numbers of lilac napkins versus peach, cornflower and rose. He thought it was fun to watch Steffi arrange silk flower centerpieces and flowers in crystal vases that she kept in the reception area, and he'd asked countless questions about catering. He'd also made the two women laugh when he'd gravely pronounced Sandi should never be a waitress again because she was so bad at it.

Now he was in major trouble and she felt it was all her fault.

She slowly rose to her feet.

"I'm asking that you not be too overly harsh with

Patrick,'' she said quietly. "I'll have my things moved out of here within the hour.''

Jack's head snapped up. He frowned at her as if she'd interrupted something important.

"What do you mean you'll have your things moved out of here?'' he asked incredulously. "If you think you're going to quit after this, you've got another think coming. You're not running out now.''

"I was hoping you'd let me quit so you wouldn't have to fire me,'' she said honestly.

His fingers tightened around his glass. He looked away, the muscles in his jaw flexing.

"I'm not blaming you, Sandi,'' he said in a low voice. "In a way, I guess I have to blame myself.''

She stepped forward until she stood next to him. She hesitantly rested her fingers on his thigh. The muscles bunched under her featherlight touch.

"Patrick's decided he wants a mother, and it appears he'll do whatever he thinks is necessary to get one,'' Jack said finally. "He doesn't seem to understand it doesn't work that way, and that saying things like what he did can only make things worse.''

"I wanted things to be better. I said it cuz Grandma wants me to go to an away school like my mom did.'' Patrick stood in the open doorway. His cheeks were blotchy with tearstains and his lower lip couldn't stop wobbling. "Away schools are really mean and they don't let moms and dads see you and you have to sleep with rats and there's bugs in your food and...'' He took a deep breath. Tears ran freely down his cheeks.

Sandi didn't allow him to finish. She raced over and scooped him up in her arms. "Did your dad ever say he wanted you to go to an away school?'' she asked, tipping her head back so that she could see his face.

His head shook back and forth.

"Did your dad tell you you'll be going to public school here in Montgomery Beach?" she persisted.

This time his head bobbed up and down.

"Didn't your dad buy a house that has a yard big enough for a dog?" she reminded him.

Patrick again nodded.

"But you told your grandma and Mrs. Montgomery that your dad and I were getting married because you were afraid they'd talk your dad into sending you to a boarding school?"

"Uh-huh," he whispered.

Jack groaned and buried his face in his hands.

"You know what?" Sandi whispered into Patrick's ear. "I think a nap would be in order for you right now. Then you and your dad can talk tonight before dinner. You can explain why you did what you did then."

He looked past her, giving Jack an apprehensive expression. His dad managed a faint smile.

"You can't tell lies, Patrick, just because you think it will make things right in your mind," he said quietly. "I want you to apologize to Sandi for what you did, and tomorrow we will go over to Mrs. Montgomery's so you can apologize to her and your grandmother. There will be no television for you for the rest of the week."

Patrick's eyes grew to the size of saucers. "But then she'll want you to send me to an away school because I lied!" he wailed. "She'll blame Sandi for me lying."

"No one is going to make me do anything and no one is going to blame Sandi for anything." Jack closed his eyes. "Trust me on this."

Sandi looked over her shoulder as she carried a tearful Patrick into his bedroom for his nap. She didn't look any more reassured than Patrick did.

To be honest, Jack wasn't all that sure of what would happen, either.

Chapter Eight

"I changed my clothes, brushed my teeth and brushed my hair," Patrick announced, sliding onto a chair and folding his hands in his lap with the air of one awaiting his execution.

Jack looked his son over with an appraising eye. He couldn't find any fault with his appearance. Red polo shirt and navy cotton shorts were clean and neatly pressed, his hair combed, face clean. He just wished Patrick didn't look as if this was his last day on earth.

"Sandi?" he called out. "Are you almost ready?"

"I'll be out in two minutes." Her voice was muffled by the closed door to her room.

"Two minutes or two hours? She couldn't be ready on time? She knew we were going over there at one," he muttered, sneaking a peek at his watch. He wanted to get this over with as quickly as possible for all their sakes.

Patrick tilted his head back and looked up at his father with dark eyes wide with apprehension and tiny lower lip quivering.

"We won't go without her, will we?" he asked, silently pleading with his father not to give a positive answer to his question.

"Only if she isn't out here in the next five minutes," he said grimly.

"You don't need to worry, Mr. O'Connor. I'm ready."

Jack spun around, tempted to tell her it was about time. His jaw worked furiously as he scrambled to come up with the right words. His temper took over before his brain could intervene.

"What the hell have you done to yourself? Have you lost your mind?"

She didn't flinch at his roar.

"I believe I am properly dressed for our little side trip," she said calmly.

Patrick stared at Sandi, then wrinkled his nose as if he'd smelled something distasteful. "You look really scary, Sandi."

Scary wasn't the word that came to mind as far as Jack was concerned. Sandi's tailored navy skirt ended just below the knee, and a crisp white blouse buttoned all the way up to the notched collar was definitely in the boring category. He couldn't believe she even owned such an outfit. She'd also swept her hair up and back in a prim French twist, and demure pearl studs graced her ears. He glanced at her shoes, afraid he might find oxfords worthy of a great-grandmother. He wasn't sure whether to be relieved her footwear consisted of navy leather flats. He felt as if his teal cotton polo shirt and khaki slacks were wild compared to the ultimate nanny uniform hiding her figure.

"Then let's get this over with," he said gruffly.

"SHE WON'T YELL AT ME, will she?" Patrick's tiny voice came from the back seat. "Or tell me she hates me?"

"Nobody is going to yell at you or hate you. Not when you're willing to tell her the truth. Believe me, Patrick, I hate doing this just as much as you do," Jack said as he steered the car down the road.

"Of course you do, Mr. O'Connor," Sandi murmured with just the right hint of deference in her voice. "This type of meeting is always difficult but also very necessary. Patrick needs to understand the consequences of his actions and take responsibility for them."

Jack flicked a searing glance at her and just barely managed not to grind his teeth.

She sat primly in the passenger seat with her hands folded in her lap. He couldn't detect a hint of perfume, and her only makeup was a pale pink lipstick, which he privately decided did absolutely nothing for her. If anything, the insipid color washed her out. Anyone looking at her now would think she was the perfect nanny. But then, maybe not. He wasn't sure, but he thought he'd caught a hint of white lace visible beneath the white cotton. At least, he hoped she hadn't also changed her affinity for lacy lingerie.

He remembered what she'd said about the dress code for her first teaching position. If he slipped one of her shoes off, would he find red polish on her toes?

"I'm going to be sick," Patrick whined from the back seat. He cradled his stomach with his arms, looking as sick as he proclaimed.

"No, you aren't. You have to do this, Patrick. Once it's over, you'll feel better," Jack told him with a firm voice.

"No, I won't," he muttered. "I'll be so sick I'll die."

Jack'd had a long talk with Patrick this morning,

explaining to the boy why lying was bad and why he needed to admit his wrongdoing. He knew it was a lot for a five-year-old to comprehend, so he tried to keep it as simple as possible. The boy had sniffed and cried and hugged his dad, vowing he'd never do it again. He just didn't want his father to send Sandi away.

Jack had no intention of sending her away.

Although, right now, he'd sure like to loosen her up a little. It didn't take a genius to figure out why she'd made the radical change. Did she honestly think someone would believe this disguise of hers?

"Tell me something, Sandi," he said quietly so Patrick couldn't overhear. "Did you remember to wear some interesting silk under that blouse that's only appropriate if you're going to meet the Queen Mother?"

Her lips moved slightly. He took heart at the hint of smile she tried to hide. "Then I'm wearing the appropriate clothing. After all, we are going to the royal castle even if we didn't receive a royal summons." Her own voice, too, was low.

Jack grinned. This was the Sandi he was familiar with. "You like to find humor in everything, don't you?"

"It makes the world a bit brighter. And easier to handle. Plus, when you're teaching five-year-old kids, you have to have a sense of humor or you won't survive. They take things pretty literal at that age, and you're never sure what they're going to come up with." She took a deep breath as she gazed at the turnoff.

"What are you nervous for?" He drove up the long winding driveway to reach the large wrought-iron gates that opened onto the Montgomery estate.

The white stucco structure with its Spanish tile roof

was clearly visible to the trio as the car moved slowly up the road. He gazed at the many iron balconies at the windows and wondered if ghosts inhabited some of those rooms. He was positive a house standing since 1906 should have a few. Not for the first time, he wondered how Dylan and Candice had fared growing up here. He silently rejoiced this wasn't the lifestyle Patrick would experience.

While his son wouldn't lack for anything, he would still have a good grounding in what was important. True, money can make life easier, but it can be gone as easily as it can arrive. What mattered most was what was inside a man. And Jack meant for Patrick to grow up to be the kind of man who had the right values.

"I'm not exactly one of Mrs. Montgomery's favorite people. I have a good idea she hasn't forgotten that Steffi and I locked Candice in the janitor's closet when she was to be presented as Spring Queen at the country club. Or the time we hung Dylan's underwear from the flagpole. Or…"

"I get the message," he said hastily, fearing what he might hear next.

Sandi shrugged. "It was our rebellious stage. We got violently ill the only time we tried smoking, drinking made us sick and we're allergic to marijuana. We had to do something."

Jack choked. "You're allergic to marijuana? You're kidding, right?"

She shook her head. "No joke about it. Our biology instructor used some for a demonstration, and we got sick the minute we smelled it burning. A doctor later verified the allergy."

"You would have made a great narc," he muttered.

Jack slowed the car to a stop at the front doors. He got out and walked around to the passenger door, opening it for Sandi. As she stepped out, his eyes swept over her. A cock of the eyebrow told her he still thought she was crazy. She merely smiled and waited as he helped a reluctant Patrick out of his seat. The boy looked apprehensive.

"It's like the times you get a shot at the doctor's office. It will be over before you know it," he told him.

Patrick made a face. "Can I have the shot instead?"

"Perhaps you'll remember this the next time you think about telling a lie," Jack said, taking hold of his hand and giving it a reassuring squeeze as they climbed the steps.

After the butler informed them Mrs. Montgomery and Mrs. Anderson were on the terrace, Jack assured him they'd find their way.

"Sure different when a wedding reception isn't going on," Sandi murmured, looking around.

"He wasn't in, so I left a message asking him to call me when he returns." Harriet's voice carried to them as they reached the open French doors. "I hope they can make it on such short notice. It's hard to say, since I don't know if Jack took Patrick somewhere or if Patrick's with his nanny."

"I've heard that Sandra is an excellent and well-respected teacher, but I honestly can't see her as a nanny. I do hope she doesn't have another agenda," Mrs. Montgomery said.

Sandra? Sandi mouthed the name and grimaced.

Jack pulled them to a stop and put his finger to his lips to indicate they remain silent and out of sight.

"I know it's none of my business, Harriet, but that

prep school I told you about would be excellent for Patrick. I wanted to send Candice to the school you sent Michelle, but the waiting list was much too long," Mrs. Montgomery went on. "Not that she didn't attend excellent schools otherwise," she hastily added.

Jack almost opened his mouth to say the school hadn't done Michelle much good, except to teach her how to think only about herself and how to be a cold-hearted trophy to a man. He wondered if that was what Grace wanted in her daughter. He didn't think Candice was everything her mother hoped for.

"Actually, her father chose that school for Michelle," Harriet replied in her soft voice. "I had another school in mind for her, but Parker felt the Davidson Academy offered the kind of education Michelle would need as an adult."

Yeah, how to shop for the very best. How to buy the very best and how to find a man to pay the bills. Jack thought cynically. *Even her trust fund wasn't enough to cover her bills. No wonder she graduated from there with honors.*

Grace said eagerly, "That's why I offered Jack my assistance when he told me he was moving here. I think it's wonderful he's relocating down here, and there is no reason why Patrick can't meet children his own age at the Bolton Academy or the Prescott Day School. Those are the type of school where he will have the chance to meet children of the right people. Men his father will associate with on a regular basis."

Jack noticed the fire raging in Sandi's eyes and had a good idea what was running through her mind. It was apparent she was ready to blow and if she did, Mount St. Helens would probably seem nothing more than a discreet burp compared to Sandi's explosion. He gave Patrick's hand a reassuring squeeze, took hold of Sandi's with his other hand and literally pulled them outside. Sandi was so startled by his abrupt gesture that she gasped. She would have fallen on her nose if he hadn't had such a tight grip on her hand.

"Good afternoon, ladies," he said jovially. "We hope we haven't come at a bad time." He released her hand and placed his arm around her waist. He squeezed tightly in warning. Her eyes flashed warning flares but, thankfully, she remained silent.

Harriet looked up, her face wreathed in a warm smile when she saw her grandson. Jack released Patrick's hand as Harriet opened her arms, inviting him to her. She chuckled at his faint grimace when she kissed his cheek, then used her thumb to wipe the lipstick smudge from his skin.

"What a coincidence you're here. I'd just called your hotel," she told Jack. "I left a message asking if you would like to join us for dinner this evening. All of you." Her gaze took in Sandi. As Sandi's appearance registered, a faintly puzzled frown creased her brow. Her smile didn't waver as she surveyed her new image.

Jack didn't miss the displeasure that faintly marred Grace's face before a bland smile replaced it. He had a pretty good idea that Grace's invitation didn't include Sandi.

As usual, Grace was elegantly dressed in pale pink raw silk pants, a matching tailored blouse and cream-colored leather low-heeled pumps. Her attention was now focussed on Sandi. There was no doubt she felt a great deal of suspicion regarding Sandi's demure appearance.

"Thank you, I accept for all of us," Jack said graciously. His fingers tightened around Sandi's waist. "Since we were going to drive over to the new house, we thought you might like to go with us."

"But, Dad," Patrick said, staring at his father with an expression that easily said he had no idea what was going on.

Jack sent his son a silencing look. "Yes, son, I know you thought we were going to do something else, but I know you want to show your grandmother your new room. I also thought it would give her a chance to get to know Sandi a little better."

Patrick let out an excited yell that had everyone wincing.

"I gather your father's suggestion meets with your approval, Patrick," Harriet said with dry amusement.

He looked at his father with a smile that stretched across his face. "Yeah, I want everyone to do everything Dad said," he said in a fervent tone bordering on awe.

Sandi thought about finding a nice quiet room where she could indulge in a very large glass of wine. Maybe two or three. Amazing, she rarely drank, but the events of the past couple of days were beginning to make it more desirable.

Jack, damn him, stood there looking as if confirming his engagement was an everyday occurrence.

As if sensing her thoughts, he tightened his grip.

"Smile," he ordered between smiling lips.

"I hope your nose grows down to your toes with all the lies you're spinning," she whispered back while keeping a smile frozen on her own face.

"If so, your pert little nose will do some growing,

too, because you're going to have to lie right along with me," he whispered back.

"What do you think you're doing?" Sandi whispered fiercely once she and Jack had a moment alone.

Jack hadn't wasted any time piling everyone into the car. He hadn't stopped chattering the entire time it took him to drive to the house.

Sandi suggested Harriet sit in front where she would be more comfortable. That way she could sit in the back seat and stare daggers into the back of his head.

He wasn't sure, but he suspected he was developing a bad headache thanks to the mental curses he was sure she was heaping on him. He knew once he could speak to her alone, he was going to have a lot of explaining, even if he still wasn't sure why he'd done what he had.

He had just, once again, confirmed he was engaged when he had no desire to get married. Sure, saying you're engaged doesn't mean a wedding will follow. Cori and Dylan were proof of that.

Now he'd done it. After his lengthy lecture to his son about lying, he'd gone and done the exact same thing. He'd have some heavy-duty explaining to do to Patrick after this.

"Are you listening to me?" Sandi whispered in his ear, grabbing his arm and pulling some of the hair on it in the process.

He hissed a curse and tried to break free. Instead of answering, he pulled her down the hallway toward the master bedroom, while Patrick happily chattered to his grandmother while showing her his bedroom and detailing how it would be a big boy's room instead a baby's room like he had in their apartment.

"Nothing more than a change of plans," he said

after he kicked the door closed behind him. He smiled as she looked from him to the door and back to him again. "I knew we would need a little privacy for this conversation, and Harriet will assume we want some privacy for other reasons. She'll keep Patrick and herself out of the way."

He lifted his hands, releasing the first three buttons on her blouse and smoothing the collar back. She batted at his hands, but he easily pushed them away. He hummed his approval at the faint hint of cleavage now displayed. But he wasn't finished.

"Will you stop that!" Sandi ordered, again trying to restrain his hands as he rolled up her skirt waistband with the ease of a man who knew what he was doing. By the time he finished, her skirt rose several inches above her knees. Still not content, he pulled her purse strap off her shoulder and rummaged through the contents.

"Do you mind?" she tried to snatch it back, but he easily held it out of her reach. "What did you have to drink before you left the hotel? And did you happen to take heavy medication along with the alcohol? I'm voting for the latter, because you are acting insane."

"No, I don't mind at all." He pushed aside a few items and pulled out a lipstick tube and small bottle of perfume. He inspected the latter first, decided the fragrance was appropriate and tipped the liquid onto his forefinger.

He slowly drew it around the soft curve of skin behind her ears and in the hollow of her throat. She stilled when his finger slowly stroked down her chest until it hovered just above the shadowy cleft of her breasts. When she looked up, she found his gaze fastened on the spot gleaming with the liquid scent drawn on her skin. He slowly lifted his gaze to meet hers. His eyes seemed to burn through her.

"This is *not* a good idea," she whispered, a combination of desire and caution written all over her face.

"Don't ever play poker, Sandi. You don't have the face for it. As for *this...this* is a very good idea. Best I've had in a long time. You're the Pied Piper." His lips were close to hers. Much too close. "The one who charms the men into dancing to her tune. Her music weaves a spell that can't be ignored. Even when she's dressed like a matron you see in one of those bad prison movies."

"I am not dressed like a prison matron!" She huffed. If she was frantic a moment ago, she didn't show it now. "All proper nannies dress this way." Her chin lifted in a manner that defied him to argue with her.

Jack hadn't gotten to where he was without plowing on through the face of defiance. And when said face looked like Sandi's, it was even easier to forge ahead.

"If this was what you wore when you taught at that first school, I'd say a great many fathers nurtured more than a few fantasies about you," he murmured.

Her eyes shot flames. "I *did not* inspire fantasies for anyone!"

"That's what you think." His finger traced the line of the collar. "Anyone who looks like you always inspires X-rated fantasies."

Her breath appeared to stop in her throat as she was caught in his gaze. "No, I don't."

Jack nodded. His eyes followed the direction of his finger as it traced the shirt collar lying flatly against her skin.

"That prim buttoned-up look would have any man

wanting to find out what's beneath all the starch and white cotton. Will he find—'' he carefully nudged the collar aside a few inches until he could see the edge of her bra ''—silk and lace or will he see something else?'' His fingertip traced the delicate lace edging. Her breathing grew labored under his touch. ''Of course, I already know your secret. Prim and proper on the outside,'' he whispered against the curve of her ear, ''sinful and sexy on the inside. Every man has dreams about a woman like that.''

Sandi was positive her heart stopped. She couldn't breathe, yet she was still standing upright, so she must be breathing by sheer will alone. No, she wasn't standing upright. Her knees were starting to turn to mush. And if she wasn't mistaken, sparks were flying between Jack's fingertip and her skin. If her heart did truly stop, there would be no problem in zapping it back to life again as long as he kept touching her.

She cleared her throat before attempting to speak. Even then she wasn't sure anything would come out coherent. She braced herself and commanded a haughty expression and glacial eye.

''Be careful, sir. I am not Jane Eyre and you are not Mr. Rochester.''

He smiled wickedly, looking very much like the Victorian figure she'd just mentioned.

''Jane was a governess to a little girl, Sandi, not a nanny to a little boy.'' Now his fingertip settled on bare skin. ''And she lived during a rigid time period. She didn't have the freedom to think for herself back then. One thing you've proved to me is that you think for yourself very well.''

The electric shock of his touch raced through her system like a live wire.

"Your...his...Patrick's grandmother," she said between dry lips. "She could show up at any moment."

Jack turned his head slightly. Patrick's excited chatter floated faintly through the closed door. "She's not here, Sandi. It's just us. Patrick's too busy showing Harriet the deck outside his room." He nudged the collar aside a bit more and replaced his exploring finger with his lips.

Sandi sucked in a breath that literally hurt her lungs. Jack's breath was hot against her skin as he leisurely nibbled a sensual necklace around her throat.

"Jack." His name drifted from her lips on a soft puff of air. She gripped his forearms for balance.

"Mmm?" He wasn't detracted from his task. "You taste very good, Sandra."

For once she didn't react to her full name. She was too lost in the heat of his kiss. "Someone could come in," she sounded desperate.

She should tell him to stop. She *will* tell him to stop. Maybe later.

Jack O'Connor was making her feel all too good from the tips of her toes to the top of her head. Or maybe it was the other way around. By now, Sandi was past caring as long as Jack didn't stop what he was doing. Yes, he definitely *shouldn't* stop.

And if he did, she was going to drag him back to her.

Her eyes drifted shut as she allowed herself to just *feel*. When cool air drifted over her chest, she thought nothing of it. When Jack's lips seemed to travel a bit farther south than expected, she thought nothing of it. When his mouth again traveled north and settled on her mouth, she did more than think about it; she kissed him back with equal fervor.

Her lips parted under his gentle assault, and she settled herself more securely in his arms as he wrapped them tightly around her.

The moment Jack's body molded against hers, Sandi knew the man was most definitely not teasing. Especially when she considered what was nudging her which told her just how serious the man was.

She could feel her insides melting and her imagination urging her on to dragging the man down to the carpet and doing unspeakable things to him. No kindergarten teacher should even be thinking of such things, but she didn't care.

He looked good, smelled better and felt like something out of one of those dreams that had her waking up ready to attack any man who dared cross her path. At least this time she had a man within reach.

Her tongue curled its way around his, enjoying his unique taste while she seemed to literally hum with anticipation. Or was that him?

"Sandi." His voice in her ear was husky with an arousal that equaled hers.

She didn't want to open her eyes. In fact, they could just stand here and keep on kissing as far as she was concerned. Was that his hand resting against her breast? That felt pretty darn good, too. In fact, way past good.

Doug never sent you into this mindless state, her brain reminded her.

Doug who?

"Sandi, you're not making it easy for me," he murmured.

She smiled, feeling more than warm and fuzzy at the moment. "Funny, I thought I was making it hard."

Jack's chuckle turned into a groan. "That, too. But

we've been away from Harriet and Patrick long enough that they might start looking for us. Think we can put this on hold for a while?''

She opened her eyes and looked into dark pools of awareness. They fairly blazed the message how much he wanted her.

This was no dream. Then Jack used his hands to gently push stray strands from her cheeks. She murmured her dismay as she felt the disarray. When she looked down to find the discarded hairpins, Jack grasped her chin with his hand and tipped it upward so she could face him.

"Leave it down," he instructed, combing his fingers through her hair. "No more uptight clothing or hairdos, Sandi. I want them to see you just the way you are. Let them see the real you. The one that Patrick adores.''

She looked down at her blouse now gaping open revealing her Victoria's Secret bra guaranteed to boost cleavage. It appeared to have worked. She fumbled with the buttons, then swore under her breath when one button ended up in the wrong hole.

Jack chuckled and swept her hands to one side. In no time, he efficiently refastened all but the top three buttons. When she moved to button those, he grabbed her hands.

"Your...Patrick's grandmother is going to know something went on here," she groused, finally giving up. "Let's not give her any ideas, shall we?"

"We're engaged, remember?" He lightly tapped the tip of her nose with his forefinger. "It's expected we'd fool around when we have a chance to be alone.''

"Not fool around so much that..." Her gaze drifted downward. "I suggest you compose yourself. Think cold shower. Think of your absolute worst date. Think of your mother standing on the other side of the door.''

Jack grinned. ''You and I making out in my room and my mother in the hall. A teen boy's dream.''

''You are impossible.''

Sandi stepped away from him and headed for the door. When she pulled on the knob, nothing happened. She looked over her shoulder and found Jack standing in the same position, grinning at her.

''You locked it.'' Her accusation lacked heat.

He walked up to her and reached around her to release the lock button. ''Of course, I locked it. I didn't want Mom barging in.'' He turned the knob and pulled the door open, gesturing for her to leave first.

Sandi looked over her shoulder as she walked out of the room.

''Now I see where Patrick picked up hints on how to be sneaky. I'm going to have to have a long talk with him.''

He rested his hand against the small of her back as they walked down the hallway.

''I'm glad to hear my son picked up all my best traits.''

''It's a lovely house, Sandi and Jack.'' Harriet walked into the living room at the same time Sandi and Jack did. ''And obviously a house meant for a family.'' Her smile encompassed Sandi.

''Not like the house Michelle grew up in,'' Jack said, but without a touch of defensiveness. More a statement of fact.

''No, not like her father's house. Parker did believe a house was meant to show a man's worth. I always felt it was the people who mattered,'' Harriet said a bit wistfully. She looked around the empty room then smiled at Sandi. "It appears you'll have a decorating job ahead of you. You must be excited to have the chance to start from scratch."

Sandi smiled back even as she mentally cringed when she noticed a grubby handprint on Harriet's pearl-gray slacks. She hoped Harriet didn't mind the dirt or say anything to embarrass Patrick. Which was why Sandi chose a work wardrobe that was washable instead of dry cleaning only. It only took one time involving a new navy wool skirt and dabs of red fingerpaint for her to realize dry clean and young children don't mix.

Harriet trailed her fingers along a wall.

"All the rooms definitely need a paint job," Sandi commented, then looked down. "New carpet wouldn't hurt, either."

"Patrick's hoping he can have a rug shaped like a race car in his room," Harriet confided.

Sandi grinned.

"I always did like challenges."

She remembered the first time she entered the house and the possibilities that sprang into her mind. Color schemes, fabrics and furnishings had flooded her senses as she thought how it could look. A home instead of a house. A place where a small child could run through without fearing he'd break something. A comfortable place where friends could gather together.

Right now, she felt she had enough to worry about. Such as Harriet looking at them closely enough and easily figuring out they weren't in the master bedroom measuring the windows for new drapes. Sandi felt new horror when she looked at Jack and noticed his hair was mussed and a hint of pink lipstick was smudged against his mouth and throat. She wasn't sure whether it was better to just die now of embarrassment or wait until later when Patrick wouldn't be around to watch.

"Dad, Grandma showed me an otter swimmin' in the ocean." Patrick ran over and grabbed his father's hand. "Come see him." He pulled on Jack's hand until the man went with him.

Sandi wasn't sure whether to beg to go along with them or stand there like an adult and make chitchat with Harriet. She opted for the latter.

"Mrs. Anderson—"

"Harriet, please." She smiled. "After all, in a sense we'll be family."

Sandi felt herself floundering. "I realize you must wish it was your daughter standing here instead of me," she began.

The older woman held up her hand to stop the verbal flow. "Please don't concern yourself, dear. I love my daughter dearly, but Michelle could never be considered mother material." Her smile was sad, showing what regrets she felt. "Or even wife material. She prefers her freedom."

It was then that Sandi began to look at the older woman through different eyes. She'd bet the farm this woman was nothing like Grace Montgomery.

"So it doesn't bother you if Jack ends up with another woman?" she ventured.

"What would bother me much more would be if my daughter had hurt Jack so much he didn't allow another woman into his life," Harriet said candidly. "He is a warm and loving man and deserves a woman who will truly appreciate him for the man he is. The best thing Michelle did was give birth to Patrick and leave him with Jack. Patrick is a warm and loving child and deserves a mother who will give him that same kind of love."

Sandi leaned against the waist-high bookshelves that bisected the living room from the family room. She rested her palms against the wood top, feeling the light layer of dust under her palms. She dreaded to think what the back of her skirt looked like.

"And what about the suggestion to send Patrick to boarding school?" she asked.

Harriet chuckled. "I was afraid you might have heard what Grace said. Especially when I saw how quickly Jack appeared on the terrace. She enjoys handing out advice, whether it's wanted or not.

"Grace doesn't realize the school my daughter attended did her nothing other than cost a great deal of money. I wouldn't have dreamed of suggesting it for my grandson, who appears to have thrived in preschool. My husband was the one who believed that the higher the school fees, the better the education. Do you plan to continue teaching after the wedding?"

"Yes," Sandi replied, keeping up the tale of the fictional engagement.

In fact, she could get into this storytelling. Surprising, since she hated Doug for letting her think she was engaged to him when he was actually engaged to another woman. "Teaching is very important to me."

"How do you do it?" Harriet asked. "How do you keep that age group in order day after day without losing your sanity?"

Sandi winked. "Handcuffs and muzzles. Sometimes cages," she confided in a mock whisper. "If that doesn't work, there's always sleeping gas. They don't have a chance."

Harriet chuckled. "I must say, you're a braver

woman than I am. I look at Patrick and I see how much energy he has, and I wonder how anyone can keep up with him twenty-four hours a day, much less fifteen or twenty more like him.''

''I used to say a couple of glasses of wine helped, but some people thought I was serious,'' she quipped. ''It's amazing how many people have no sense of humor.''

''Then Jack must be a challenge for you, since he's always so solemn.''

Sandi was puzzled. ''Solemn, Jack? Oh, I've listened to him talk to clients, but he never seemed solemn to me.'' *And he'd been far from solemn when they were alone in the master bedroom.*

''He does seem freer than he has been in some time, which I have to credit you with,'' Harriet said. She likewise leaned against a shelf, seemingly not caring that dust would get on her outfit.

She was surprised by the woman's sincerity. ''Thank you, but I think it's Patrick who keeps Jack from the grumps. Sometimes I have to remember which one is the kid.''

''I'm glad to hear that.''

Sandi mentally patted herself on the back for keeping up a good impression. Jack hadn't come out and said it, but she sensed he feared Harriet would try to come between him and Patrick. Either that or the woman was an incredible actress and hoped to catch Sandi off guard. Not that she was paranoid or anything.

So why did Sandi have the urge to assure her she never had what it took to pose for *Playboy?*

Chapter Nine

Sandi's brain refused to shut off as it ran at warp speed.

Could Harriet think their engagement was a sham and be trying to trip her up? It would be something Grace Montgomery would do. She knew just how sneaky that woman could be. Which was why it was well-known that every year Grace Montgomery never worried about competition for the presidency of the Ladies League. Sandi knew Grace wouldn't allow it. Just as she almost didn't allow it when Cori announced she wasn't going to marry Dylan, and that Dylan was marrying Whitney Emerson instead. While Whitney was a wonderful woman and clearly loved Dylan, she knew Grace didn't consider the young woman a social equal. Sandi was glad Dylan was the type to stand up to his mother and marry for love instead of social prestige.

Then she reminded herself that Harriet seemed to be a good friend of Grace's. Maybe there was something redeeming about Grace after all. Harriet seemed like a good woman.

"Well, what do you think?" Jack said a bit too

heartily when he and Patrick came back into the living room.

"It's a lovely house, Jack. I'm sure once you've all moved in, it will truly become a home," Harriet replied, smiling at both of them as Patrick ran over to her and allowed himself to be hugged. "You're very lucky that Sandi and Patrick get along so well. Be careful, my dear. Perhaps she's marrying you for your son." She chuckled.

Jack glanced at Sandi, who merely smiled. He had to look again, as if unsure just exactly where that smile was coming from.

"I always did think Patrick had all the looks in the family," Sandi joked.

"I guess we should be returning Harriet to the house before Grace sends out a search party," he said, keeping his tone hearty although it sounded a bit forced by now.

"Honestly, Jack, you talk as if I were a stray puppy." Harriet looked amused. "I realize Grace isn't one of your most favorite people, and I'm grateful you're willing to spend the evening with us."

"Puppy?" Patrick perked up, then grinned sheepishly when his father shot him a telling look.

"Mrs. Montgomery is a bit…" Sandi paused, trying to choose her words carefully "…overpowering at times."

Harriet shot her a wry glance. "Overpowering? My dear, Grace has a spine made from pure tempered steel and a stubborn streak to match. She also plays a mean game of bridge and canasta, and I'm positive she cheats. I've just never been able to catch her at it. Still, her cook makes the best lemon soufflé I've ever tasted. I've tried to steal her away for the last twenty years and have failed every time.'' She walked over and put an arm around Patrick's shoulders. ''Come, dear, you can show me the backyard again, where you plan to play with your puppy when you get one.''

Jack groaned as grandmother and grandson walked out of the room.

''Why did she have to use that word? I wanted to wait on the puppy,'' he muttered.

''Grandmothers always get their way, don't you know that?'' Sandi teased, threading her arm through his. ''C'mon, Dad, let's get out there before they decide to stop off at the animal shelter on the way back to the Montgomerys'. With Grandma present, Patrick might think he can talk you into anything.''

Jack groaned again as Sandi dragged him outside.

''I promised him a dog. Isn't that enough?''

''Of course it isn't, silly! Not when you're five years old and even a few minutes' wait seems like an eternity. You know what?'' she said, looking up at him with an impish smile. ''I think this engagement could be fun.''

Jack's head snapped around and down. His eyes held a bit of suspicion in them as he stared at her. He was trying to gauge what she was up to. She was the picture of innocence.

''You know what men say about women like you? 'Be afraid. Be very afraid,''' he told her.

She couldn't resist hugging him with her free arm. ''But that's what makes me so fun, sweetheart,'' she cooed.

''Can we go look at puppies, Dad?'' Patrick asked as they climbed into the car.

''Not today, Patrick,'' he answered as he backed down the driveway. ''Until we move in, we don't have a place to keep a puppy. The hotel doesn't allow pets.''

Patrick looked ready to argue. ''But I saw that man with a dog when we had breakfast.''

''Sweetheart, that man is blind and his dog helps him not bump into things and helps him cross the street. That dog is very special,'' Sandi said gently. ''Besides, wouldn't you rather wait until you're in your house, where your puppy can play in the yard instead of being cooped up in the suite?''

''Maybe he could stay with Steffi,'' he said hopefully.

''Steffi isn't all that fond of dogs,'' she explained. ''Or maybe I should say, her cat isn't fond of dogs.''

''How does the fiancé feel about cats?'' Jack asked.

''Greg gave Trika to Steffi, so there's no problem there.''

Patrick wrinkled his nose with distaste. ''You can't play ball with a cat,'' he grumbled. ''Or take him down to the beach and play.''

''Cats have never been fond of water,'' Harriet agreed. ''You'll love a puppy much more, dear. They love little boys, while cats merely tolerate the human race.''

SANDI DIDN'T FEEL as apprehensive this time when they arrived at the Montgomery house. She noticed Patrick seemed more cheerful. That worried her, because she feared that Patrick thought his lie was turning into a truth. She wondered how Jack would explain to his son this engagement wasn't real. And how Patrick would feel when he heard it.

Even worse, how was Jack going to explain why it was all right for him to lie but Patrick shouldn't do it?

After they entered the house, Harriet excused herself to go upstairs and freshen up for dinner. Grace directed Sandi to a guest bathroom so she could do the same.

Sandi didn't miss the woman's eagle eye taking in the abrupt change in her appearance compared to her ultraconservative look when she'd arrived earlier that afternoon. She grasped Patrick's hand and escaped to the bathroom with the explanation that Patrick needed to wash his hands and comb his hair.

"Sandi?" Patrick wiggled his fingers under the flow of warm water. He giggled when she handed him a thin sliver of guest soap shaped like a swan. "Do ya think Dad's not mad at me anymore for what I said yesterday?" He'd carefully omitted the word "lie" from his question as if not saying it meant it didn't happen.

"I don't think he's angry with you, but I do think he might be disappointed in you," she replied, pulling a fluffy burgundy fingertip towel off the rack and drying his hands. Once finished, she carefully combed his hair. She took a quick look at her back, noticed the dust marring the navy surface and brushed it off as best she could with her hands. "You have to be careful what you say, because lies can hurt people. Your grandmother seems like a nice lady, so I know you won't lie to her anymore, will you?"

He looked shamefaced. "I won't." He hugged her tightly. "I love you, Sandi." His voice was muffled against her skirt. "And I'm glad that Dad said you're going to marry him."

"I love you, too, tiger," she murmured, dropping a kiss on top of his head.

Before she opened the door, he tugged on her hand. She looked down.

"I just wish it was true that you were marrying my dad," he said wistfully.

Sandi looked into his dark eyes, so like his father's, and felt herself fall in love with the son.

"Don't you know that saying, Patrick? 'Be careful what you wish for,'" she murmured. She left the rest of the words unsaid. She thought his wish sounded pretty good to her.

DINNER PROVED TO BE less stressful than Jack had anticipated. Truth be told, he even found himself relaxing, and not just because of the excellent wine Grace served with the meal.

At first, Grace was a bit stiff with Patrick. He guessed she wasn't used to having a small child at the dinner table. But Patrick with his natural charm, soon had her smiling and laughing at his nonsensical jokes. He was pleased to see that Patrick remembered his table manners. He couldn't help but notice that Sandi had polished the boy's manners even more. Even to where he remembered to use his napkin as a napkin and not as a handkerchief.

Jack thought this would be good practice for Grace for once Dylan and Whitney's baby was born. He wondered what kind of grandmother she'd make. He could never fault Harriet as a grandmother. When she'd discovered Michelle was pregnant, she'd never once suggested Michelle and Jack get married or applied any other kind of pressure. Instead, she'd warned him she wanted to know her grandson, and she would be the kind of grandmother who enjoyed spoiling her grandchild rotten. And in many ways, she had been the kind of grandmother every child should have.

Except now Jack worried that the older woman might have something else in mind. Since Michelle was her only child, and she had frequently voiced the fact that there would be no more children, Patrick would be Harriet's only grandchild.

The mouthwatering roast lamb suddenly tasted like ashes in his mouth. He kept an eye on Patrick when his son used both hands to pick up the crystal goblet holding his milk. Luckily he was equally careful placing it back on the table. Sandi wiggled her nose at Patrick, who thankfully took the hint and wiped his upper lip clean with his napkin. He grinned proudly.

"Harriet said the house you chose is quite lovely. And on the beach." Grace commented.

"With a backyard for a puppy," Patrick announced.

"What kind of puppy do you want, Patrick?" Grace asked. "I know of several dog breeders in the area who might have the kind of dog you want."

"We're going to look at the animal shelter," Jack interjected. "I'd prefer we give a homeless dog a home."

"And I'll take care of the dog all by myself." Patrick puffed up with self-importance.

Grace smiled briefly at the boy. "Dylan wanted a dog when he was just about your age. Unfortunately, we had to say no because he was going off to school the next year. His father was also allergic to dogs."

Patrick looked first at his father then at Sandi. Apprehension was written across his expressive features. Sandi smiled at him.

"Since Patrick will be attending the local school, he'll have plenty of time to learn how to take care of his dog," she said softly. "I understand there's even special classes for children to learn how to properly care for a puppy."

His head bobbed up and down. "A big one." He held his arms out.

"Let's not think of a dog as something to ride, tiger," Jack said dryly, picking up his glass of wine and taking a healthy sip.

"I'm also going to get a bed that looks like a race car," Patrick announced, starting to bounce in his chair, then quickly subsiding under his father's chastising eye. "And I can pick it out myself!"

"The furniture in my apartment isn't suitable for the house, so I'm going to sell the apartment furnished," Jack explained.

"Makes the move a lot less stressful when you don't have furniture to worry about," Sandi quipped.

Jack leaned back a bit as the butler refilled his wineglass. "There's still the china, the silver, crystal, our personal belongings, my art collection and Patrick's toys."

"China?" she said faintly. "Crystal? Art collection?" She sincerely doubted his idea of an art collection involved velvet paintings or a collage of Gary Larson cartoons plastered on a lampshade, like the one her class had given her for Christmas one year.

"Jack has an extensive collection of Impressionists," Harriet said enthusiastically. "Some have been on loan at various museums."

Sandi was right. The caricature done of her last summer wouldn't fit in at all.

"Isn't your sister marrying soon?" Grace asked Sandi.

"Yes, she is," Sandi replied, coming out of her

reverie. "Steffi has been keeping doubly busy between planning her own wedding and her catering business."

"Where is she having the ceremony?" Grace asked as she buttered her roll.

"In the Bower Chapel's garden, then the breakfast reception is being held in the hotel's ballroom. They're having a dawn wedding."

Both women stared at her. "A dawn wedding?" they said in unison, for once letting their surprise show.

Sandi nodded. "Steffi wanted their marriage to start off at the beginning of the day. She checked the *Farmer's Almanac* and decided the ceremony will be at 5:30 a.m."

"Good luck getting the nonmorning kid here," Jack said wryly.

"I think that's a lovely idea your sister wanting to start their new life together at the beginning of the day," Harriet said. "It's just a shame it has to be held so early in the morning," she chuckled.

"Steffi is very much a morning person," Sandi explained. "Whereby I'm a night person. I'd be better off staying up the night before."

"I suppose you would then prefer a midnight wedding," Grace commented with a tiny wrinkle of her nose, indicating neither would be her idea of a proper wedding ceremony. "Mimosas would naturally be served at hers, but champagne and hot chocolate don't seem like an ideal combination."

Sandi seemed to consider the idea. She opened her mouth to reply, but someone answered for her.

"She can't have a middle-of-the-night wedding," Patrick piped up.

Grace raised an eyebrow at his impudence.

"And why ever not?" she asked frostily.

He looked at her wide-eyed, as if the reason was only too apparent. "Cuz I'm not allowed to stay up that late."

"I'D SAY THAT MADE for an interesting evening," Jack said wryly.

Sandi looked over her shoulder to note that Patrick was slumped over, sound asleep in his seat.

"I guess that means you're not voting for a midnight wedding," she joked.

His arch of the eyebrow was every bit as frosty as Grace's had been earlier.

Jack had been glad that with Patrick present they'd had an excellent excuse to escape early.

After that all too short a time in the master bedroom, he'd discovered he wanted more time alone with Sandi. The taste of her mouth was addictive, and she felt like heaven in his arms. He wanted that again.

Once they reached the hotel, Sandi herded a sleepy Patrick into his room, while Jack checked his messages.

He made notations as to the importance of each call and set the list aside to make his callbacks in the morning. As he made notes, he could hear faint sounds coming from the bedroom—Patrick's sleepy voice and Sandi's murmured replies.

He got up and walked into the bedroom. Sandi was sitting on the bed with her back against the headboard. Patrick was cuddled up next to her with his head resting against her breasts so he could read the book along with her. He could see Patrick's mouth silently forming the words.

He rested his shoulder against the doorjamb, his

hands in his pants pockets as he listened to the soothing sound of her voice. He was intrigued by her ability to alter her voice to fit the different characters.

She'd changed her clothes and now wore an ankle-length, tank-style cotton knit dress the color of a ripe tangerine. Since her feet were bare, he could see that her toenails were a brilliant orange color. Her hair was caught up in back with a clip, but stray strands fluttered around her face. There was nothing of the prim-and-proper nanny he'd seen earlier. This was the Sandi Galloway who'd fascinated him from the beginning.

Why had he continued Patrick's lie?

He could have nudged his son out onto the terrace, silently prompted him to fess up and get it over with. He could have made his own apologies, said goodbye, and that would have been it.

The rational part of his brain told him Harriet wouldn't try to take Patrick away from him. She was a nice lady, pure and simple. He'd always felt she was too nice. Nice as in unreal. Especially for a guy like Parker Anderson. The man was as hard-nosed as they got and the total opposite of Harriet. Yet, she'd worshiped the man.

Maybe that had been the problem with him and Michelle. He'd thought Michelle was like her mother. It hadn't been long before he'd found out otherwise. She'd turned out to be as hardheaded and focused as her father.

Until then, he'd had no idea love could be blind.

He watched Patrick's eyes droop until they finally closed and didn't open again.

Sandi's voice softened until she was barely murmuring. As if sensing Jack's presence, she looked up.

She was smiling at him, and what he saw was pure heaven.

She looked down at Patrick, who slept in her arms.

"Tomorrow he'll inform me I didn't finish the story," she whispered, carefully disentangling herself from the boy and laying him back on his pillow.

Jack walked up to the bed and bent over, dropping a kiss on Patrick's forehead.

"You have a great kid," she told him.

"Yeah, I know." He stared at his son, feeling the love well up inside him. "When he was born, I wondered if I could be a good father. Did I have it in me? I had this tiny baby looking to me for everything, and I felt as if I had no idea what everything was."

She smiled at his confession. "I'd say you've done all right. I've always felt a person is either a natural parent or not. They're not made, they're born. And you are definitely a natural. Patrick is so well adjusted, it's downright scary."

Jack looked pleased by her praise. "We had a crazy time during those terrible twos, but he snapped out of them around about his third birthday. And now—" he looked down at his son again "—I feel as if he's suddenly grown up overnight. One day he was happy just sucking his toes, and the next he's talking about being a race-car driver."

"Next he'll tell you he wants to be a doctor or a lawyer." She walked over to him and tucked his arm in hers as she guided him out of the room. After making sure the night-light was on, she carefully set the door ajar. "Although, since his afternoon at the bakery, he's decided he wants to be a baker."

Once out of the room, Jack took over. He slid his

hand down her arm and grasped her hand. He gave it a gentle tug as he headed for the open patio door.

"Come on. The moon is full, the night is young," he began, steering her toward a chair. "And the wine is ready." He gestured to the open bottle and two glasses sitting next to it. He poured wine into the glasses and handed one to her. He held his own glass up high in a toast.

"To a lady who's got more sheer nerve than anyone I've ever known," he announced before lifting his glass to his lips.

Sandi sipped her drink. She found the wine held a hint of tartness that tingled on her tongue. She took another sip because it was easier to concentrate on her drink than look into Jack's eyes. Eyes that were saying a great deal. Her entire body tingled with the answer he wanted.

Jack took the glass out of her hand and set it on the glass-topped table.

"Feel better?"

She looked at the glass then up to him. "You choose very good wines." *That was a scintillating line, Sandi! What are you going to say next? Ask him what his birth sign is?*

His lips twitched with a hint of a smile as if he read her thoughts.

"I'd hoped I'd chosen one you'd like." His hands rested lightly on her shoulders. His gaze swept her from the top of her head to her toes. "Now you look like the Sandi I know."

She flicked the full skirt with her fingertips. "Nothing unusual."

"After today's performance, yes, it is very unusual and very nice," he crooned, trailing his hands down her arms until they reached her wrists. He clasped them with his fingers. "This is what I like to see." He bent his head and sniffed the soft skin of her throat. "And smell."

She took a deep breath. "Likewise. You know," she pulled her wrists back until her fingers could lace through his. "We're not locked in the master bedroom now."

He grinned. "No, we're not. Great, isn't it? You, me, a bottle of wine, a beautiful night, the ocean be-low—" he nodded behind him "—soft music. Every-thing we need."

Sandi purposely looked over the railing. "At least no dead fish have washed ashore," she quipped.

He shot her a look that said he wasn't buying her act.

"There's also a sleeping kid nearby," she reminded him while she still had a few brain cells functioning on a responsible level.

"A kid who sleeps like the dead the minute his head hits the pillow and doesn't wake up until the next morning, when getting him up is like waking a log." He nuzzled the soft spot just behind her ear. His breath was warm against the supersensitive skin.

She could feel oxygen leaving her brain. Making it impossible to think. Especially when his lips made a moist trail behind her ear.

"Jack," she whispered.

"Sandi." Her name was a prayer on the wind just as his mouth claimed hers in the kind of kiss she saw in movies. A kiss that took away all thought and san-ity. A kiss that, as far as she was concerned, should never end.

Chapter Ten

Jack knew that Sandi's kisses were pretty spectacular, but tonight's were going way past spectacular and well on into impressive.

Her lips were soft and yielding under his, parted just enough so his tongue could slip past and discover her distinctive taste blended with the wine into an intoxicating mixture. Her soft moan that ended with his name was just as intoxicating.

"Did anyone ever tell you that you are one very exciting woman?" he rasped, drawing back long enough to take a breath.

She looked up with eyes hazy with desire.

"Not lately," she replied, her voice barely there.

He slid one finger under a strap and gently pushed it down her shoulder.

"No strap lines," he murmured, following the downward slide with his lips.

"Jack?"

"Hmm?" He pushed aside the dress bodice to reveal a pearly white breast that clearly had not seen the sun. "No topless sunbathing?" he asked just before his lips fastened on the rose-colored nipple.

"Ah" was all she could say as the fire raced from

her nipple to her womb. Jack gently blew on the moist skin, sending molten lava right after the fire. She gripped his shoulders because her balance was gone. Her universe centered around the lips against her skin and the hands that roamed her now bare shoulders and breasts as her dress fell to her waist. She brought herself back to the present long enough to pull his polo shirt out of his slacks and draw it over his head. She had no idea what direction she tossed the shirt and she didn't care. She felt her dress being tugged down lower.

"I think I should warn you that I didn't bother with any underwear tonight," she whispered.

His hands stilled. He looked up, an eyebrow arched in such a way that warned her she was playing with fire again.

"I bet you ran with scissors as a child, didn't you?"

"Only when I didn't get caught." She looked around. Luckily, theirs was the only balcony facing this side. "And speaking of caught, helicopters have been known to fly by around this time of night and sometimes a hot air balloon. I don't know about you, but I know I wouldn't like to be a part of anyone's vacation pictures."

Sandi was positive her skin was humming. Then she realized that it was Jack chuckling against her throat.

"That would be interesting," he said as he stepped back. "Do you think they'd go for photos or slides?"

She could feel the laughter bubbling up. "Don't make me laugh, Jack."

"After such a heated moment, I wouldn't dream of it." He bent his knees and before Sandi was aware of his intentions, she was in his arms. "I vote for privacy." He carried her into the parlor, slid the patio door closed and walked into his bedroom. A sweep of one hand and the lamps by the bed issued a soft light to the room.

Still cradled in Jack's arms, Sandi looked at the king-size bed dominating the large bedroom. The rich ruby silk quilted spread gleamed like a jewel against the erotic backdrop of black lacquer furniture. The same brilliant colored silk covered a chaise and a chair set in a corner, while the wall behind the headboard echoed the dazzling hue.

"Oh my." The two words were issued with awe as she stared at a room that seemed to have been specially made for lovemaking. She twisted her neck so she could see the entire room. "This isn't anything like my room."

"Good thing it isn't, or I might have been tempted sooner." He walked over to the bed and slowly lowered her to her feet. He held up his palm to ask for silence, then walked out of the room.

Unsure of how this was going to proceed, Sandi hastily pulled her dress up and straightened the straps over her shoulders. She sat on the bed, pushed herself back and arranged herself in a provocative position against the pillows. Quickly deciding it was *too* provocative, she slid forward until she reached the end of the bed. She dropped her legs over the edge and crossed them with the uppermost foot nervously swinging to a melody only she could hear. She was ready to bolt off the bed and head for the chair when Jack appeared in the doorway.

He was still bare-chested when he walked into the room. One hand held the bottle of wine and one glass. He used his foot to close the door behind him. He set the bottle and glass on a nearby table and refilled the glass. He carried it over to the bed and held the rim against Sandi's mouth. She smiled tentatively before parting her lips and sipping the liquid flowing over her lips. When she drew back, he lifted the glass and pressed his mouth to the same spot she'd drank from. At the same time, his eyes focused on her face. She looked up at his face and sensed the flood of heat across her cheekbones.

She might as well have been reclining against the pillows in that first provocative position. Her flushed face told him all he needed to know.

"No tourists flying by," he murmured, setting the glass to one side. He took her hands in his and pulled her to her feet. "No hot air balloon floating by. Not even a seagull."

This was it.

This wasn't Doug, whose idea of romance had been jumping naked out of the bathroom with a big leer on his face before giving her a deep-throated kiss.

This was Jack, who seduced her with fine wine, sexy words and an even sexier body. Jack, with the look in his eye that she knew had to be echoed in her own.

God help her. She was going to make love with a man who had to be heaven on earth.

GOD HELP HIM. He was going to make love with a woman who was the most beautiful creature he'd ever seen. A woman who made him laugh. Who loved his son as much as he did. A woman who had captivated him from the first time he'd seen her filching gingered chicken off a buffet table.

She wore bright colors that rivaled a rainbow. He'd swear her toenails were painted a different color every day, and she was the most unorthodox nanny and kindergarten teacher he'd ever come across. Not that he'd met many.

She looked up at him with hazel eyes that gleamed with a dazzling gold of desire. Her lips were moist from the wine and her breasts rose and fell with increasing rapidity. She gestured to her surroundings with a motion of her hand.

"I feel as if I were a slave girl brought in from the harem to please her master," she said in a husky voice. "You have to admit, the ambience lends itself to the idea."

"An interesting scenario," he agreed. "And what would the slave girl do to please her master? From what I've heard, if she didn't please him well enough that night, she could die in the morning, couldn't she?"

The wicked gleam in Sandi's eye told him she'd read his mind perfectly. With her usual grace, she stood up. A hitch of each shoulder brought the dress straps back down her arms, baring her breasts. She held her head high, a smile on her lips that dared him to say something. When he didn't, she pushed the dress downward until it fell around her ankles in loose folds. She stood naked before him, obviously proud of her ability to arouse him.

The scant white patches of skin stood out starkly against her light tan, except for the reddish-brown patch of hair at the apex of her thighs.

"Does this slave's appearance please her master?" she asked in a low voice. While the words inferred deference, the haughty expression on her face was the exact opposite.

"Very much," he said once he'd recovered his vocal chords. "Except I appear to be overdressed." He gestured to his slacks.

Without a word, she reached over and unclasped his belt. She unthreaded it from the loops and dropped it to the carpet. She then unfastened the button and lowered the zipper with agonizingly slow motions.

Jack gritted his teeth against the exquisite pain of her hands on his bare skin as she just as slowly pushed his pants and briefs down to the carpet. Her demeanor wasn't that of a slave trained to please her master, but of a woman secure in her own femininity, ready to please the man she'd chosen to give herself to. What started out as a game was developing into something that fairly sizzled between them.

Sandi's look was bold as she gazed down at his arousal.

"I guess we'll have to think about doing something about your problem." She turned away, then pulled back the bedspread and top sheet. When she bent over to accomplish her task, Jack pulled the clip from her hair, allowing it to tumble down around her face.

"This is how I like to see your hair. Wild and free," he murmured, bunching the tangled curls in his hands and bringing them to his face. "Smells like coconut."

"The shampoo I use has coconut oil in it," she said softly.

"It makes me think of a tropical island. You, me. Naked."

She looked over her shoulder and uttered a muted laugh. "You do have a fixation on nudity, don't you?" She twisted so she could sit on the bed. She drew her legs up to curl beside her body. She looked up at him and held out her hand.

Jack bent one knee onto the mattress and leaned

over her even as her arms linked around his neck and drew him down to her.

"I was so nervous," she whispered as his lips feathered over hers.

He looked quizzical. "You, nervous? I couldn't believe you'd be nervous about anything."

She hesitated. "Let's just say my one foray into romance wasn't what it was supposed to be, though I pretended it was. I'm already seeing the difference, and this is definitely the better. I just don't want to disappoint you."

Jack brought her hand to his erection, which pulsed under her caressing touch. She curled her fingers around the silky smooth skin that seemed to grow even larger. At the same time, he curved his hands under her neck and held her head fast as he captured her mouth with his. He seemed to draw her into him as he feasted on her mouth, laving her lips with his tongue and gently nipping the corners.

While he sated himself on her mouth, she moved under him and wrapped her legs around his calves so he couldn't move away. She drew back enough to trail her mouth along his shoulders and up to the hollow of his throat. She ran her hands over the slightly rough contours of his face as if she were blind and needed to record every feature to memory.

Jack's words were dark and sexy, rough with feeling as he praised her body, praised her beauty and praised her soul. He inhaled the scent of her skin, warm with a floral note accented by the scent of her hair. He tasted her. Loved her.

When he bent his knee between her legs, they parted allowing him to cradle his hips against hers.

"Something tells me the master is now the slave,"

he murmured against her lips just as he plunged into her silken sheath that lovingly accepted him. He slid his hands under her buttocks, tipping her up for better penetration that brought a startled, and excited, cry from her lips. She assisted him by wrapping her legs around his hips as her arms circled his shoulders.

Jack had been careful with relationships since Patrick's birth. He'd refused to bring other women into his life, because he hadn't wanted his son to have an unending procession of "aunts." Not that a parade of women through his bedroom had ever been his style. At least not since college, when hormones ran high and wild.

Not even Michelle, the woman he'd thought he'd truly loved, gave as freely and joyously during their time together as Sandi gave to him their first time together.

When Sandi started writhing in his arms, he reached down between them and touched her silken folds, rubbing his thumb against the pink nubbin that released any inhibitions left. She reared up and he kissed her deeply to silence her cries as he felt himself explode.

Exhausted to the point of bonelessness, Jack rolled over onto his side and brought Sandi with him, nestling her against his side. She draped one leg over his thighs and an arm lay limply across his damp chest. He gathered up enough energy to pull the sheet back up to shield her from the evening breeze coming in through the open window before he slipped out of bed. While up, he pulled back the drapes and kept the sheer panels covering the window. When he returned to bed, Sandi automatically curled up against him.

She yawned.

"I have to say, Mr. O'Connor, you do have a wonderful sense of timing,'' she said before drifting off to sleep.

JACK KEPT HIS ARM AROUND her shoulders as she lay her head in the hollow of his shoulder. He usually didn't like a woman draped over him as he slept. It was different with Sandi. He wanted her as close to him as possible. Content, he closed his eyes and soon fell asleep.

Jack wasn't sure what woke him up, unless it was the sense that he was alone in bed. He opened his eyes and found Sandi gone. A glance at the clock told him Patrick wouldn't be up for well over an hour. He swore the kid had an alarm clock in his brain that he could set at will. He climbed out of bed and walked into the bathroom. He hoped he'd find Sandi there, perhaps luxuriating in the scandalous ebony sunken tub, but no such luck. He quickly showered and dressed in a pair of shorts and a T-shirt before he went on his search.

It didn't take him long to find his quarry. Sandi was on the balcony, frantically moving seat cushions, even looking behind the potted plant that stood in one corner. Her hair looked as it had when he'd combed his fingers through it, and her dress was wrinkled.

"What are you doing?" he asked, unable to understand the cause of her dismay.

She jumped up and smothered her shriek with her hands.

"I picked up the clothes off the floor," she whispered. "Then I realized your shirt wasn't in the bedroom. I remembered taking it off out here." She blushed. She looked around with frantic movements. "But I can't find it!"

Jack moved in closer. Before she could say another word, he dropped a light kiss on her lips. When they parted, he immediately took advantage and deepened the kiss. By the time they drew apart, both were breathing deeply.

"Jack!" she looked behind him.

"We've got an hour," he reminded her.

"I still need to find your shirt." She had a little reminding of her own to do.

Jack dropped his arms. He knew when to back down.

"Okay, I'll help you look."

"That's just it! I've looked everywhere," she told him. "It's not as if there's a large area to search."

Jack turned in a slow circle. He had to admit, the teal cotton would stand out against cement and chairs and chaise lounges with taupe cushions.

He had no idea why he walked over to the railing and looked downward. When he did, he leaned over the railing farther.

"What?" Sandi asked. "What's wrong?"

His shoulders were shaking when he gestured for her to come to him. When she reached his side, she realized he was laughing. He pointed down.

Sandi followed the direction of his gaze and gasped in shock.

The last thing she expected was to see a bright splash of teal lying by the swimming pool.

Jack took her arm and spun her around.

"How will we explain this?" she asked, once again frantic. And even more embarrassed. "What will the hotel staff think?" She suddenly moaned. "I went to school with the concierge."

"Then there's only one thing to do." He marched

her back inside. Keeping one hand on her arm so she couldn't escape, he picked up the phone and punched in the number for Room Service. "Yes, this is Mr. O'Connor in suite six-twelve. I'd like a pot of coffee and some breakfast rolls sent up immediately please. Thank you." He hung up. "Now, go take your shower, and when you come out, we'll have some coffee and rolls while waiting for the slumber bug to get up insisting he's starving." He dropped a quick kiss on her nose. "Then we're going furniture shopping."

Sandi didn't appear mollified. "Furniture to go with your Impressionist art collection?"

"No, furniture to go in the house. The artwork will just cover the walls. They're not the least bit comfortable to sit on. Now go." He couldn't resist patting her on the fanny as he nudged her in the direction of her bedroom. She shot him a warning look over her shoulder as she hastily made her escape.

Jack watched her enter her room, look at the pristine bed and quickly muss up the sheets.

Half femme fatale. Half demure.

What kind of woman would he see next?

"WE'RE GOING TO GET my race-car bed today!" Patrick hopped his way to the car. Now that he'd been fed, he was ready for his adventure.

"We'll sure look for one," Jack promised. As they walked, he wrapped his arm around Sandi's shoulders. When she looked up at him, he grinned. "We have to keep up appearances, don't we?" he whispered.

Patrick spun around and stared pointedly at the way their hips bumped companionably as they walked and at his father's arm around Sandi. He didn't say a word, but the wide grin on his face said it all.

"If you find him that race-car bed, he'll be the one who's your slave for life," Sandi told Jack.

"As far as keeping one of my two slaves in bondage, I'm afraid you've won that honor," he whispered in her ear before he tucked her into the passenger seat. Her blush was a good enough answer.

He had an idea he was going to enjoy this day a great deal.

SANDI THOUGHT OF THE ONE time she and Doug had gone out together to buy a new couch. They couldn't agree on style, fabric or even wood trim. In the end, Doug had thrown up his hands, informed her it was up to her and stormed out of the store. Since she feared the purchase would also end up on her charge card, she'd been extra cautious in making her choice.

Jack was cautious, but it was clear price was no object.

His first purchase was Patrick's new bed. It was red and blue with the form of a race car, and the little boy was ecstatic. Especially when they found race-car sheets to match. Within an hour, Patrick's bedroom furniture was chosen and a delivery day and time was arranged. At the same time, Sandi made a list of what accessories would be needed to finish the decor.

She stood to one side as Jack looked over office furniture and chose what he would need for his home office. She admired his choice: a heavy-duty old-fashioned rolltop desk that had been updated with space for a computer and telephone. She could already visualize it set in place and Jack there working. The idea was tantalizing.

"Household is next," he warned her.

"You're doing fine," she assured him, silently

groaning at the idea of entering another furniture store. "I'm anxious to see you finish the task."

"Oh, no, milady, you have to do your part, too." Jack pulled her along. "A woman's touch is always needed."

Sandi was speechless as she was soon surrounded with furniture styles and books of fabrics. And flattered that Jack asked her advice every step of the way. She admitted to herself that she knew how she would like to see the house decorated, but she had never imagined Jack would consult her.

She was surprised she didn't feel shy around him after the previous night. Still, there had been her panicked search for his polo shirt. She was still horrified that she'd accidentally tossed it over the railing. When they'd gone downstairs for breakfast, she'd pointedly not looked in the direction of the swimming pool. She didn't even want to think what the hotel staff was saying about that discovery!

"All I want is a comfortable couch that will hold up if Patrick decides to use it as a trampoline," Jack told her.

"I would hope he wouldn't dare think of such an action." She fixed a warning stare at the boy.

Predictably Patrick looked sheepish as if he knew they'd guessed his intentions much too soon.

"I can't jump on my bed, either."

"Very good." Sandi dropped her hand on top of his head.

"Then can I have a trampoline in the backyard?" he asked his father.

"Not in this lifetime," Jack muttered, studying a book of fabric swatches. He made a face and glanced at Sandi. "Choose one."

She took just as much care as she had choosing her own couch. A couch that had ended up with way too many cigarette burns because Doug had never bothered to notice where the ashtray was. She'd arranged to ship the couch to the "happy couple" as an engagement gift.

After a great deal of deliberation, Sandi chose a navy and oatmeal nubby fabric for the casually styled and sturdy family room couch, with a solid navy easy chair and hassock, and another chair in the solid oatmeal fabric. For the living room, she went with a more formal style of a mauve, blue and light green floral against a pale gray background. The chairs were in a coordinating pattern. Tables and lamps were next, and she even found a vase that coordinated with the couch. Caught up in the buying frenzy, she soon added items for the family room, found a dining-room table and chairs that Jack and Patrick thought was perfect and a table and chairs for the kitchen.

"You'll still need all sorts of linens, and kitchenware, and you'll need to decide whether you want shutters, miniblinds or drapes," she said, furiously writing in a notebook.

"Think the kid can stand it all today?" Jack eyed Patrick, who was wilting more by the minute.

Sandi dampened her enthusiasm when she looked at the boy. "I think lunch would suit him a lot more."

"We're going to eat now?" Patrick asked with a hint of a whine in his voice.

"Yeah, slugger, we're going to eat now." Jack notched his elbow around his son's neck and drew him against his side. "At the rate Sandi's getting the house furnished, we're going to need all the energy we can get."

"And a puppy?" Patrick looked up with eyes that resembled a lost puppy's.

"After the house is furnished." Jack glanced at Sandi over the top of Patrick's head. "Seems we have a couple more rooms to work on."

"Really?"

"Such as, the master bedroom." His smile was pure wolf, and his gaze as wicked as they come. "And the other bedrooms, of course."

Sandi's smile was that of an enchantress as she took a page from his book.

"I have an idea that particular task could end up to be an interesting project."

IT WAS DECIDED anything packed in the car would be dropped off at the house. Jack had called a security company earlier that day, and they had arranged to be there late that afternoon to install a security system. He dropped Sandi and Patrick off at the hotel before driving over to the house.

"I want to go, too," Patrick demanded as Jack let him out of the car. Sandi placed her hands on his shoulders.

"No, you stay with Sandi," he ordered as he climbed back into the car. "I'm going to be busy for the next few hours and you'd just be bored."

"No, I wouldn't!"

"We'll be fine," Sandi told Jack.

"I'll call if I'm going to be too late for dinner, so the two of you can go on without me," he replied. His eyes told her he wanted to touch her, kiss her, but he wouldn't do it in front of Patrick.

Her eyes told him she wanted him to touch her and kiss her, but it was best he didn't.

For now.

Chapter Eleven

"You're not planning another last-minute change of brides, are you?" Jack joked. "Here, you might need these. Or maybe I should give them to Whitney." He held up a pair of handcuffs. "I'm sure she could find some use for them."

"Ha, ha. You're a riot, O'Connor." Dylan glared at him. He snatched them out of his friend's hands.

"I guess you changed your mind about them after all," he quipped.

"Just show me the ring," Dylan demanded.

"Patrick has it all safe and sound. Don't worry about it."

Dylan nodded, still looking distracted. "Easy for you to say."

"She's not going to run off, Dylan," Jack told him in a gentler tone.

"I know. It's just…" He held up his hands in a helpless gesture.

"Hey, you're marrying the woman you love. That's what counts." Jack's eyes drifted downward. "Your mother let you out of the house wearing those shoes?"

Dylan looked down at his feet. While his tuxedo was stark black with a snowy-white shirt, his shoes were purple Creepers. The tennis shoes seemed to have a life of their own.

"They're for Whitney," he muttered. "She understands."

"She'd have to, since we both know Grace won't." Jack looked around the small room. "Let's see. You don't need to hear *the talk* since it's obvious you already know about that."

"You should talk." Dylan appeared only too happy to turn the tables on his friend. "There's been a lot of talk about you and Sandi Galloway. I even heard a rumor that the two of you are engaged. Of course, since one of the people mentioning that little bit of gossip was my mother, it has to be a lot more fact than fiction. She said Harriet was pleased to hear that Patrick would be getting a mother."

Jack was very involved in making sure his cuffs were straight.

"Jack."

"We're keeping it quiet. There's enough weddings going on right now, what with yours and Sandi's sister's coming up soon. And there's the house getting furnished and, before we know it, Patrick starts kindergarten."

"Then he'll be entering grade school, then high school and, later on, college. Try again."

Jack was spared from answering when the minister came in and announced it was time.

"Steady, old friend," Jack whispered, clapping his friend on the back. "They say after the initial shock, numbness sets in."

"I'll remind you about that when it's your turn," Dylan said out of the side of his mouth as they walked into the chapel.

Dylan's nervousness disappeared the moment Whitney, on Karl's arm, started down the aisle.

The groom gazed at his intended with open love as she walked slowly toward him in a gown she'd designed especially for the occasion. A rich cream color, the corset-style top dipped to a deep V in front, with the full skirt floating down to her calves and cut to masquerade her pregnancy. Her hair, pulled up in curls, was decorated with sprigs of baby's breath. The rapturous smile on her face was obviously meant for Dylan alone. There was no doubt this couple was meant for each other.

Grace Montgomery, dressed in a pale lavender dress, sat in the front row. Her expression could be described as stoic at best.

Jack noticed that when she turned her head to view the bride, her expression changed. He wasn't sure exactly what he was seeing, but he sensed that something Grace saw brought a softening to her heart. He hoped that meant she would give her new daughter-in-law a chance.

He knew Grace's marriage hadn't been a happy one. If Dylan had married Cori, he would have most likely ended up in the same kind of unhappy marriage his parents had had. Unhappy because they were the wrong ones to be united. Luckily Dylan could never be the coldhearted bastard his father had been.

As Jack stood there, he could see Patrick proudly bearing the pillow holding the wedding bands. And he could see Sandi seated several rows back. Her smile broadened as she watched Patrick's progress. And her smile grew a bit secretive when she looked at Jack.

There's mischief in those eyes, he thought to himself. *What is she up to?*

Random thoughts ran through his mind. The first one set him back on his heels.

For some very odd reason, Jack wondered if she was wearing underwear. Not exactly an appropriate thought to be having during a wedding, but he was fast discovering that thoughts about Sandi weren't all that normal.

Her smile deepened.

Now he knew he was right.

He took deep breaths and tried to think about anything but her. He kept his attention on Whitney and Dylan, listened to Karl announce he was the one giving Whitney to Dylan, and that he expected Dylan to take good care of her. Karl stepped back and sat down next to Grace.

Dylan's quiet assurance that he would protect her with his life brought sighs from the female guests. More than one woman looked at Jack, as if gauging whether he would give that same vow toward the woman he'd choose.

Jack made a promise to himself to disappear when Dylan threw the bride's garter.

"You can't take the rings! I hafta protect them!" Patrick shouted, pulling the pillow from Jack's reach.

"It's okay. I have to give them to Whitney and Dylan, son," he whispered, keeping his arms draped over his son's shoulders as he untied the ribbons holding the rings.

"Then why'd I have to be so careful with them?"

"I knew he was too young to do this properly." Grace's voice could be heard in an undertone.

"I wouldn't worry, Grace. A perfect wedding is not as interesting as one that has one or two minor mishaps that brings a smile to one's lips,'' Karl murmured.

After the minister pronounced Whitney and Dylan man and wife, Dylan didn't need instructions to kiss the bride. He swept her into his arms and kissed her long enough to bring a blush to her cheeks and a glow to her eyes.

When Jack walked back up the aisle, he sneaked a quick glance at Sandi. She smiled and crossed her legs.

He just knew the reception was going to be pure hell.

Sandi hadn't planned on attending the wedding, but she hadn't been able to refuse Whitney. Especially after the woman had informed her that a pregnant woman's wishes shouldn't be denied.

After Jack and Patrick had left for the chapel, Sandi had pulled out a coral slip dress with matching lace bolero and had gotten herself ready. She'd winced as she'd slipped on her matching high heels, which she knew would leave her feet aching long before the day was over.

As she'd dressed, she'd recalled she'd spent a great deal of money on the outfit for a dinner party she was supposed to have attended with Doug. In the end, she hadn't gone, and the dress and shoes had been relegated to the back of her closet.

Jack had never seen her dressed up, and she wanted to show him that casual wasn't the only style she knew. Judging from the interested looks she'd received from the male guests, her outfit was just right.

At the reception, she stopped in the ladies room to freshen her lipstick and dab a hint of perfume behind her ears and in the hollow of her throat.

She'd barely walked into the room where the reception was being held when she was grabbed by the hand and drawn against a hard male chest. She recovered her wits quickly enough as she was swept onto the dance floor.

"If you wore that dress to make me crazy, you've accomplished your mission," Jack murmured, his lips hovering next to her ear. "Considering the close fit, I have to wonder what you're wearing underneath it."

She gazed at him with wide-eyed innocence. "Why, Mr. O'Connor, are you asking me if I'm wearing any underwear?"

Luckily her question was meant for his ears only.

"There's quite a few men looking at you as if you're the main course." He shot one such man a warning look as he approached them to cut in. The man hastily backed off.

"That's funny, I would have thought I'd be considered more a dessert than an entrée," she mused as he guided her around the dance floor. "My, my, you are hungry, aren't you?" Her eyelashes dipped to shelter the wicked gleam in her eyes.

"You can be assured, we'll continue this conversation later."

Sandi grinned. She'd never thought of herself as a sensual woman, but something about Jack brought out a side she hadn't known existed. Perhaps it was because he made her feel fully like a woman, and she wanted to show him just how much of a woman she was.

"I am sorry, Jack, but you cannot keep this lovely woman to yourself." Karl tapped him on the shoulder.

Jack gave her a smile of apology and relinquished his hold.

"You look lovely today," Karl told Sandi.

"Thank you, sir." She adopted a coy smile as she dipped her head in response to the compliment.

"And Jack has not been able to take his eyes off you, which is as it should be. You make a striking couple."

"The nanny and the millionaire has already been done, Karl," she reminded him.

"I do not think he sees you as a nanny but as a very desirable woman. Perhaps that is why the two of you became engaged."

Sandi was spared a denial when a man cut in. She was never so grateful for an interruption, because she had no idea what she would have said to him.

When the time came for toasts, Jack presented the first one.

"To Whitney and Dylan," he pronounced. "May they have a long life together, many children, especially daughters that will turn Dylan gray long before his time," he joked, "and may their love continue into eternity."

Sandi lifted her champagne glass as the others did, then drank.

It was the kind of toast she would have wanted at her own wedding. Just as long as Jack was the groom.

"ONE WEDDING DOWN, another to go." Sandi breathed a sigh of relief as she slipped off her high heels and massaged her aching feet. "I sure hope Steffi's goes as smoothly as Whitney and Dylan's did. Wasn't it sweet of Harriet, offering to take Patrick to dinner? I swear he looks so grown-up when he's in his tuxedo." She winced as she rubbed her sore toes.

She groaned happily when Jack lifted her feet into his lap and began kneading her instep. "Forget any interview. You've got the job. That feels so good,'' she said with a moan.

"Now I wonder where I've heard that before,'' he teased as he continued massaging her feet.

"I haven't danced that much in ages.'' She pointed and flexed her toes a few times then wiggled them. "I don't think I'll be walking anytime soon.''

"Don't worry, you'll be up and running in no time,'' he assured her, trading one foot for the other.

"I swear, high heels were invented by men to make women cripples.''

"High heels were invented by men, because they make a woman's legs look sexier.''

"Then more men should wear high heels and they'd understand what we go through,'' she groused.

"Sorry, hairy legs and heels just don't do it for me.''

Sandi grabbed the dangling ends of Jack's bow tie and pulled his face toward her.

"Do not make jokes when sore feet are involved.'' She enunciated each word with deadly precision.

He shook his head. "You are one dangerous lady when you want to be. I think I better get your mind off your feet.''

"Good luck.'' The words barely left her mouth before he framed her face with his hands and kissed her with a deep hunger that definitely had her forgetting all about her aching feet.

Not that she had to worry about being on them for a while.

"I WANT TO HEAR ALL ABOUT your engagement to Jack O'Connor and I want every decadent detail!''

Steffi pounced on her sister the moment Sandi entered the catering office.

Sandi raised her eyes heavenward at the sound of her twin's demanding voice. Since she'd just spent the morning directing the placement of the master bedroom furniture and linens, Jack was more than on her mind. And not as her boss, either. "Who told you?"

"Who told me? *Who told me?* Just about everyone in town except for my sister, who should have told me before she went around telling everyone else!" Steffi flung her arms out, the picture of a injured sister.

"Let's see, where should I start? Not to mention talk about you and him at Whitney and Dylan's wedding. But let's start with the engagement news, shall we?

"I-first heard it from Heidi when I stopped by the florist shop. Then David at the bistro. Thea at the chocolate shop also told me. And Melanie at the bakery." She ticked each one off on her fingers.

"Along with an interesting tidbit from Donna at the inn about a man's polo shirt being found near the swimming pool. Coincidentally, it was found pretty much under your balcony." She eyed her sister with something bordering on amusement. "Care to tell me about that stunt?"

Sandi could feel her face reddening. She would never forget Jack's amusement at the idea of his shirt being thrown so haphazardly over the balcony. "I have no idea what you're talking about." She affected a haughty manner as she reached out and straightened the collar to Steffi's bright turquoise polo shirt that was tucked into black twill walking shorts. The name of the catering company was embroidered in pink on the turquoise fabric.

"Oh sure, that's what everyone says when they're caught," Steffi muttered. "First you're working for the guy and, suddenly, he's bought a house and the two of you are engaged. You didn't go anywhere near that fast with Doug the Worm."

Sandi shifted uneasily under her sister's keen gaze. "Doug believed in taking things slow and easy, and I admired him for his patience. That and the fact that he respected me so much. Little did I know his patience had more to do with his trying to keep two women happy at once," she admitted.

"So what exactly *is* going on?" Steffi asked as she walked back to her desk and sat down. "And why didn't you tell me about all this in the beginning? Everyone assumed I knew all about you and Jack O'Connor and here I am totally clueless." She pouted.

"You have enough with your own wedding to worry about," Sandi reminded her, positive it wouldn't deter her twin for long. "Besides, it's a very long story that I will tell you after you've survived your wedding. I'm just surprised nothing's shown up in 'Cami's Column,'" she added, referring to a social column featured weekly in the local newspaper. She inwardly shuddered at the idea of Cami Lawrence eagerly telling her "devoted readers" the truth.

Especially if the truth had to do with Sandi Galloway. Cami had a habit of carrying grudges. No matter that Sandi hadn't known that Cami hadn't officially broken up with Brad and had been merely making him suffer by telling him she never wanted to see him again. He'd recovered from the break-up in no time— just in time to ask Sandi to the Valentine Dance and she'd accepted. Cami had never forgiven her. Even if Cami had won in the end when she'd married the faithless Brad right out of high school. No one was surprised when she'd ended up divorcing him after six years of watching him chase after high school seniors because he'd refused to grow up.

Steffi eyed her knowingly. "Cami would kill to get any dirty tidbit she could on you. I ran into her at the produce market a week ago, and she asked me why your hunky attorney fiancé wasn't with you. She also wondered about your new job as nanny and if you had quit teaching. If she thought you were engaged to someone like Jack O'Connor, she wouldn't be giving you a moment's peace."

Sandi groaned. "That woman is the worst kind of busybody." She stared at her sister through slitted eyes. "What did you tell her?"

"I told her he fell into the bay and was suing the State for a dangerous environment and that you're doing the nanny bit as a favor for the Montgomery family."

"You're kidding?"

"No! Even wilder is that she believed me! Even the bit about doing a favor for the Montgomerys!"

The two sisters erupted into laughter until they had to wipe the tears from their eyes.

"Your message said you picked up my gown when you picked up yours," Sandi said in hopes of averting her sister's attention from any more questions about Jack.

Luckily it worked. Steffi walked over to an old-fashioned amoire, threw it open and drew out a plastic-bagged gown.

"Heather picked hers up, too. I can't believe how perfect they are!" She beamed. Her smile dimmed as she paused and practically mashed her face against the mirror beside the amoire. "Does my face look red to you? I wonder if I'm getting a rash. Does this look like a rash?" She used the fingers of her free hand to wander over her cheekbones and chin.

"Do not mention rashes!" Sandi shouted at her. "I refuse to have some kind of rash all over my face while wearing a pink gown." She took the bag from her sister and unzipped the heavy plastic covering. She admired the pale pink silk gown. "Is the veil in here, too?"

She nodded. "The shoes won't be ready until this afternoon. I confirmed our hair appointments, and Heather will meet us there."

Sandi winced at the idea of wearing high heels yet again after so many months of sandals and running shoes. Except Steffi wanted a formal wedding, including shoes manufactured to torture the female foot. She privately vowed to kick them off the moment the ceremony was over before she ended up injured.

"Since you're having a dawn wedding, it didn't seem very practical to have a bachelor party for the groom or a bachelorette party for the bride the night before the wedding," Sandi told her with the warm loving smile that always had Steffi bristling with suspicion. "But I was able to arrange something special."

Steffi looked wary. "Why does this worry me?"

"Jack said there's no problem with my having the evening off before the wedding. Or should I say two evenings before the wedding." Sandi looked smug. "Don't worry. Transportation will be provided, so none of us will end up in jail for wild behavior." She slung the bag over her shoulder. "Love ya, sis."

"Sandi! What kind of party are you talking about?" Steffi demanded.

Sandi looked over her shoulder as she opened the door. "The kind you'll never forget."

"Sandi."

She turned around.

Sandi couldn't deny her sister was in love. It fairly radiated from Steffi. And Sandi could understand why. Steffi and Greg had been dating for the past four years. They were ready to make their commitment to each other, and Sandi was positive their relationship would last because their love was a lasting one.

She ached for that kind of love.

The last few days with Jack and Patrick had been the kind that created memories. Jack had already told her he had plans for the next morning that didn't include work. That they wouldn't be alone didn't bother her. She'd already lost her heart to Patrick and having the little boy with them made those times more special, even if all they did was walk along the shoreline and explore any tidal pool they came across.

Sandi hadn't returned to Montgomery Beach with thoughts of looking for another relationship. Not with Doug so fresh in her mind. She didn't want any kind of relationship this fast. But then she hadn't planned on meeting Jack, either.

Steffi's smile never wavered. "I love you, too," she murmured in a sardonic tone.

"You're going to love this party." Sandi blew her a kiss as she sauntered out of the office.

Chapter Twelve

When Sandi walked past Karl's shop, she noticed the man was standing near the window. She smiled and waved with her free hand. He smiled back and gestured for her to come inside.

"Coffee and macaroons," he told her, taking the plastic dress bag from her and hanging it on a nearby hook. Out of habit, he lowered the zipper and inspected the gown. "You'll look lovely in it."

Sandi made a face. "I just wish Steffi had picked a color other than pink. I'm going to feel like a display of cotton candy."

"It's not that shade of pink," he pointed out, holding a bit of the fabric between his thumb and forefinger. "I have seen roses this delicate shade. Think of yourself as a rare bloom."

"Funny, I usually see this delicate shade in the candy aisle." She collapsed in one of the comfortably plush chairs with her tanned legs stretched out in front of her. "I have this nightmare that the hairdresser will mistakenly put a chemical on my hair that will turn it the same color pink, then the color will extend to my face so I match all over."

"Now you're thinking like your sister," he chided.

"She's already working on a rash," Sandi told him. "A rash that I will inherit, since that's the way it seems to work." She picked at a loose thread hanging from her shorts.

Karl noticed her movements, grimaced and swiftly came over. He produced a pair of shears and snipped the thread free.

"And here I thought you knew better. You could unravel a hem or seam that way." He carried the errant thread over to a wastebasket and dropped it in. "I hope you do not do that with your gown." He picked up the thermal carafe and poured coffee into two china cups. He carried one cup and a plate of macaroons over to the table by Sandi then returned for the second cup. He took the chair nearby and sat down. "Here you are involved in your sister's wedding, when it might not be long before you will be planning your own."

Sandi closed her eyes and groaned.

"That is not usually the response someone hears when a wedding is mentioned," Karl said, picking up the plate and offering her a macaroon.

She picked one up. "Weddings can be so complicated. Steffi got on my case for finding out from pretty much everyone in this town who obviously knew before she did."

"I did not see an announcement in the newspaper," he said, taking a macaroon for himself.

"We're holding off making it super official. There's so much to do right now. Steffi's wedding, the new house, getting it furnished and all," she babbled. "School for Patrick starting before you know it."

Karl smiled. "If a wedding is desired, everything else will pale beside it. I understand Patrick is very eager to have a mother. Especially if that mother is you.''

"Patrick wants a mom who'll make him brownies and who smells good," she replied.

"Even then he would want someone who would love him and his father.''

Sandi grew very interested in her macaroon as she nibbled around the edges.

"You really need to get a love life of your own, Karl,'' she grumbled. "Then you wouldn't have to worry about anyone else.''

He merely smiled.

"BOY, IT'S REALLY PINK, isn't it?'' Patrick studied the gown Sandi hung on the bathroom door. "Like strawberry ice cream. Huh, Dad?'' He looked over his shoulder.

Sandi turned around and found Jack leaning against the doorjamb, his hands in his pants pockets. He straightened up and walked over to them. Just as Karl had done earlier, he fingered the silky fabric.

"Strawberry ice cream. Good enough to lick,'' he murmured, casting a glance in her direction.

She arched an eyebrow and did her best not to let him think he could embarrass her.

"Be careful, or I'll redecorate your bedroom in this color.''

"Only if the nightgown you're wearing is this color,'' he said for her ears only.

"I'm sure glad I don't have to wear a pink tuxedo,'' Patrick piped up. "It's really a girl's color, isn't it?''

"Not always,'' Jack told him.

"I'm still glad I'm not wearing a pink tuxedo,'' Patrick declared, bolting out of the room.

"You are really pushing it, mister," Sandi warned, poking Jack in the chest with her forefinger.

He captured her punishing finger and brought it to his mouth.

"What color do you call this?"

She breathed in sharply as his mouth closed around the digit. "Peacock."

"Hmm, the name seems contradictory."

"Only you would think so." She used her free hand to pat his cheek. "Your son is nearby, O'Connor. Behave."

"I do. Very well, I might add."

Sandi zipped the bag shut and carried it over to the closet.

"You still don't mind that I need the night after tomorrow off?" she asked.

"Of course not. I'm going to take Patrick out for a hamburger and a Disney film. It took some doing, but I finally made him understand the party you're going to is for girls only and he wouldn't have any fun." He frowned as he studied her face. He placed his hands on her shoulders, rubbing them lightly. "Sandi, you're not a slave here. Your sister's wedding preparations are important, and I told you you could have all the time you needed."

She shifted uneasily under his touch. "People know."

"What?" He cocked his head to one side.

"People know," she said in a louder voice but still barely above a whisper.

"Know what?" he whispered back.

"About—" she cleared her throat "—about the shirt."

"What about the shirt?"

She refused to look at him. "About the shirt ending up by the pool."

"Sandi, it's not as if there was a tag inside with my name on it."

"They still know it had something to do with us," she insisted with a trace of hysteria in her voice and manner.

"Only if one of us told anyone, and I don't think that's something either of us would have done," he countered, moving his hands to roam slowly up and down her back. By the look in her eyes, she was starting to relax. He only wished he could relax her even further, but with Patrick wide-awake in the next room, it wasn't a good idea.

"I have an idea," she murmured.

Jack moved in closer, nestling his hips against hers. "So do I."

Sandi chuckled. "My idea is a little safer than yours."

"But not as much fun." He rocked his hips against hers in blatant invitation.

"Down boy."

"Easier said than done, gorgeous."

Sandi rolled her eyes. "The man gives out compliments. What do you want?"

"What do you think?" His leer was well past suggestive.

She placed her palms against his chest and pushed him back. He grinned, not the least bit insulted by her rejection.

"Heather left a message that everything is ready for Steffi's party, including Sean." He flashed her a suspicious gaze. "I'm curious. What does Sean have to do with the party?"

Sandi grinned. "He's going to make the party really fun by jumping out of a cake. You know all about that, don't you? The entertainment jumping out of a cake at a bachelor party?"

"I guess that's something I missed."

"Yeah, right."

He chose to ignore her skepticism and changed the subject before he got pulled into dangerous territory. "You'll be ready to move into the house day after tomorrow? You won't be too fatigued by the party? And Sean?"

She groaned. "Ha, ha, very funny, O'Connor. Now, get out. I want to take a shower. *Alone.*"

"Pity." He made a great show of closing the door after him.

Sandi heaved a big sigh as she went into the bathroom and turned on the shower.

"Pity is right."

SANDI WAS SURPRISED when Jack offered to provide the limousine for the bride-to-be and her attendants the night of Steffi's bachelorette party.

"Considering the way you're dressed, it's probably a good idea you'll have some protection," he told her, openly admiring the bronze velvet dress that floated around her ankles. Jack was relieved to notice the deep-set lace V-neck was backed by nude-colored fabric, though he still feared it would attract too much attention.

"I could get used to this kind of service," she joked as the driver assisted her into the roomy interior of the car, while Patrick *oohed* and *ahhed* over the stretch limo.

"Just no jumping into the cake with the entertainment," Jack reminded her.

"They're gonna have cake?" Sandi could hear Patrick ask as the driver closed the door. "Sandi, can you bring me some cake?" he shouted after her.

"This is fantastic!" Steffi laughed hours later as the champagne flowed freely and a near-naked man wearing an emerald sequined G-string undulated in front of her. His bow tie hung around her neck, and a pair of men's bikini underwear lay in her lap.

Sandi whooped when Sean danced his way past her to their friend Heather, one of Steffi's bridesmaids, who blushed as he pulled her to her feet and bumped his hips against hers. One of the other bridesmaids also jumped to her feet and began dancing with him.

"I swear, if Greg's bachelor party is anything like this, I'll kill him," Steffi declared, even as her champagne glass was refilled. She didn't notice that her silk dress had hiked up a few more inches as she shifted around in her chair.

"I wouldn't worry, Stef. I doubt they'll have anyone like Sean at Greg's party," Sandi said glibly.

"You know, you're right," Steffi said in a less-than-steady voice.

At least it sounded unsteady to Sandi.

She picked up one of the crab puffs arranged on a plate in the center of the table and brought it to her lips. Since the world was starting to look a bit fuzzy around the edges, she decided some food would be in order. A second and third crab puff followed the first, but that only made her hungrier. After that, she began trying the other tidbits. She tapped her foot against the floor in time with the rousing beat of the music.

Steffi threw her arms around her twin. "Thank you, Sandi. This is one party I'll never forget!"

She hugged her back. "Good, because you're only getting one bachelorette party to go with your one marriage. Four more days of freedom, Stef. Live it up now."

After the party the women were too hyper to settle down. Sandi persuaded the driver to cruise the beach. The women piled out of the limo to run barefoot on the sand with the wild abandon of five-year-olds.

By the time the women were delivered to their prospective homes and Steffi was tucked into her bed, Sandi was feeling no pain. She floated through the lobby and upstairs, content with the rose-colored fog surrounding her. She hummed to herself as she slid her key card into the slot and waited for the light to turn green. Mindful of the late hour, she crept into the darkened parlor and carefully closed the door after her.

She jumped, covering her mouth with her hands, when a light suddenly blazed.

Jack sat in a chair by the lamp he'd just turned on.

"Have fun?" he asked mildly, taking in her disheveled appearance and slightly swaying figure.

"Fantastic." She drew the word out. "Sean was double-jointed." She uttered the acknowledgment as if it was the most important thing in the world.

"Obviously a useful skill in his line of work." He stood up and walked over to her.

"Obviously," she agreed. "You know, this was the first bachelorette party I've ever planned, and it went great. Everyone had a lot of fun. I think Heather gave the limo driver her phone number. I think she gave it to Sean, too." She leaned over and started to slip off her shoes. She would have fallen on her nose if Jack hadn't been quick to grab her.

"I can see you're going to be a lot of help tomorrow," he murmured, guiding her into her room. He nudged her arms upward and efficiently divested her of her dress and slip. He groaned when he saw the low-cut bra and high-cut panties that matched her dress, not to mention a lacy garter belt. He wasted no time in unhooking her bra and dropping a nightgown over her head.

"Who turned out the lights?" she grumbled, fighting the soft cotton folds as they covered her face.

"It's better that way," he muttered, slipping off the garter belt and silky hosiery. By the time he had her in bed, he was breathing hard and not because of exertion. "Go to sleep. We have a busy day tomorrow."

"Jack, are you double-jointed?" she asked in a sleepy voice.

He paused at the door. "No, but I don't think I need to be. Good night."

"Night."

"I should be nominated for sainthood." He closed the door and went to his own bed. After a very long and very cold shower.

"SANDI, DADDY SAID YOU'D want these." Patrick shook two small plastic bottles in front of her.

She moaned and pressed her fingertips against her temples. "Patrick, please don't do that," she whispered.

"Sandi, are you sick?" he also whispered as he carefully set the bottles on the table. One bottle toppled over.

Sandi moaned again. "Just a headache, sweetie."

"Daddy said to take four aspirin and four vitamin C. Sandi, why are you wearing sunglasses inside?"

"Because my eyes are trying to jump out of my head," she admitted in a soft voice.

"Good morning, sunshine."

Sandi whimpered and jumped at the same time.

"Please don't shout."

"Blueberry pancakes!" Patrick yelled with glee as he hopped into his chair.

In deference to Sandi's delicate condition, Jack had ordered from Room Service. So far, she stuck to drinking black coffee while valiantly ignoring the aroma of eggs, sausage, pancakes and orange juice.

She made her way gingerly to the table set up on the balcony, then promptly complained that the seagulls were too loud, the sun was too bright and the clouds too fluffy. Jack moved the food inside, and a puzzled Patrick finally sat down to eat.

"Patrick, if you'd like, you can take your breakfast into your room and eat it there while watching cartoons," Jack told his son.

The boy didn't waste any time carefully carrying his plate into his bedroom, then coming back for his glass of milk.

Jack moved over to the bar.

"Here, try this." A glass was thrust under Sandi's nose.

She stared at the red, and what she thought was green, contents and tried not to gag.

"You'll feel better once you've drunk this," he assured her.

"I don't think so." She grimaced and turned away.

"Believe me, Sandi, it will help." He waved the

glass under her nose. "It's a time-honored remedy. Just down it as quickly as you can."

Sandi took the glass and took a tiny sip. She made a rude noise.

"Just drink it." He used his thumb and forefinger to hold her nose closed.

She swallowed the contents of the glass and gagged.

"That was disgusting!"

He wasn't the least bit sympathetic. "It's better than suffering a hangover." He pushed a plate of scrambled eggs in front of her. "Now eat this."

She quickly ate the eggs, hoping they'd kill the horrible aftertaste of the concoction Jack made her drink. She tore off her sunglasses and glared at him.

"You are a very mean man."

He chuckled. "I hate to tell you this, sweetheart, but bloodshot eyes trying to give a look meant to kill a man in his tracks just don't cut it."

Sandi closed her eyes. She could swear she could see the red lines decorating her sore eyeballs. "I told Steffi I'd give her a party she'd never forget. Something tells me I won't forget it all that easily, either."

Chapter Thirteen

After hanging up her clothing in the closet, Sandi wandered through each room in the house so she could view the decorating scheme as a whole.

Everything worked as she'd hoped, with the final effect being a home meant for a boy to bring his friends to play. She stood off to the side and watched delivery men bring in Jack's art collection, which had been carefully crated for the move.

"No velvet paintings of Elvis?" she quipped, catching a glimpse of colorful shapes that made no sense to her.

"That one is in a museum," he replied.

"I hope the artwork doesn't feel the decor is beneath it." She tried to peer past the protective covering.

"Artwork is like basic black. It goes with everything." Jack left her side momentarily to direct the delivery men as to where to leave the rest of the paintings. "You've done an excellent job with the house."

She looked a bit embarrassed. "I tried to make it comfortable for you."

His gaze on her was warm. "You did."

Sandi smiled. "Then I did my job."

Jack looked around, noting the throw pillows on the couch that invited a person to lean back against them. Large silk flower arrangements on either side of the fireplace lent color and warmth to the brick. Everywhere he looked he found personal touches Sandi had added to make each room comfortable and inviting to anyone stepping inside.

"I didn't see any signs of alphabet blocks, finger-paint easels or flash cards anywhere," he told her.

"Then you must have missed the master bathroom. I also added 'Sesame Street' decals to the sliding glass door, so you don't accidentally run into it."

He draped his arm around her shoulders and walked around the room. "You are so good to me."

They walked downstairs to the other bedrooms.

Patrick was happily occupied putting his toys away on shelves painted bright blue to match his race-car bed with its coordinating sheets and bedspread. Even his toy box was shaped like a race car. Primary colors were splashed on both the wallpaper and the coordinating border.

Sandi was pleased with the final effect and what pleased her even more was Patrick's obvious delight with his new bedroom that reflected his growing self.

The guest room she'd taken for her own was decorated in calming shades of lilac, soft aquamarine, pink and mint depicted in lazy swirls on the quilted comforter with a lilac eyelet bedskirt. The colors were repeated throughout the room, creating a calming feeling.

The other two rooms were decorated in brighter colors closer to the jeweled hues of emerald and navy in the master bedroom. She walked through each room, pleased with what she saw.

Now all that had to be done was to add Jack and Patrick's personal treasures to make the house truly theirs.

She couldn't help it. She wished the house was truly hers, too.

"CAN WE GO LOOK AT PUPPIES now?" Patrick asked as they feasted on a lunch of pizza Jack had bought. He started to pick off the pieces of green pepper, until he realized his father was watching him. Instead he grinned broadly, picked up his slice and bit into it. He chewed vigorously.

"We should get settled in first," Jack said, concentrating on his own slice of pizza.

The boy remembered to wipe his face and hands with his napkin.

"But we got everything here, don't we? You said when we moved into the house, we could look for a puppy." His face twisted with his distress.

Jack looked at Sandi, who bestowed a bland smile on him.

"You did say something along those lines," she murmured, pulling a pepperoni slice off her pizza and popping it into her mouth. "There's no guarantee he'll find what he wants right away."

"I'd like that in writing, please." He sighed heavily. "All right, we'll go to the shelter this afternoon and look at the puppies. But that doesn't mean we'll come home with one," he warned.

Patrick's face split in a wide grin. "I'll find my puppy. I know I will."

Jack looked at Sandi with an expression that looked very much like desperation.

"As long as we have plenty of newspapers, we'll be fine," she assured him.

The first thing Jack noticed when they arrived at the animal shelter was all the pens holding dogs of every breed imaginable and many more who couldn't swear to one particular paternity.

Patrick looked around then looked up at his father. "Daddy, can we take them all home?" he pleaded.

Sandi squatted down on her heels and rested her hands on the boy's shoulders. "If we did that, a lot of little boys and girls wouldn't have a chance of finding a dog for themselves," she explained. "We don't have room for them all, Patrick. Just remember what I told you. Let them talk to you. And you know I don't mean talking the way we talk. They'll talk to you so you'll hear them deep inside you. You'll know when you've found the puppy that was meant for you."

He nodded. "I'll let them talk to me," he promised.

Jack followed his son closely, anticipating having to explain why every puppy here shouldn't wind up in their yards. He was surprised when Patrick stood in front of pens and made eye contract with each and every animal. He studied each puppy but declined offers to hold one. As Jack looked around, he felt the same distress Patrick had displayed when they'd first entered. The sound of barking as the dogs noticed them assaulted their eardrums and made it difficult to hear each other. They walked down the cement walkway that was still damp from being hosed down recently.

Jack noticed all the dogs looked healthy and well cared for. Some of them played with puppy toys, while others were more interested in watching the visitors.

"This shelter has an excellent reputation for finding

homes for the animals,'' Sandi murmured as if she could read his thoughts. ''They take as many as they can to certain pet stores on the weekends and have even held adoption days in the park.''

''Uh-oh.'' Jack watched his son, now seated cross-legged in front of a pen. His tiny hand was pressed against the wire mesh, while a black nose pressed against the fence from the other side.

The look on Patrick's face was pure love.

''I think a dog spoke to him,'' Sandi said, sounding almost apologetic.

As they grew closer, Jack got a better look at the dog that fascinated his son so much.

''I'd say it's more horse than dog.''

Patrick looked up when he heard their approach.

''Daddy, this is Duffy,'' he announced. ''He wants to come home with me.''

''I see.'' Jack looked at the dog, who looked back with trusting brown eyes. He wasn't totally sure, but he had an idea the dog was a lively mixture of German shepherd, Labrador retriever and a few other breeds known for their large size. He guessed the dog would tower over his son.

''Duffy's great with kids, Mr. O'Connor,'' the attendant assured him. ''The previous owners are in the military and were transferred out of the country. They couldn't find anyone to take Duffy mainly because of Megan.''

''Megan? There's two like him?'' Jack asked.

The attendant laughed. ''No, luckily there aren't two of them, although I wouldn't mind it if there were, since he really is a sweetheart. Look over in that corner and you'll see Megan. She shouldn't be in here, but they're pretty much a pair, and Duffy's a lot happier with Megan there.''

Sandi curled her fingers through the wire and peered closely into the dim interior.

"Megan?" she called out softly.

Megan lifted her head and stared at them with a great deal of disdain. The sort of disdain only a cat can conjure up. Amber-colored thick fur declared her to be royalty of the feline world.

"No way," Jack pronounced. "The dog, okay. But no cat. Cats are not my favorite animal."

"But, Dad!" Patrick hopped to his feet. "They're really good friends. Duffy can't come without Megan."

"What about a puppy? I thought that was what you wanted," Jack said.

The boy shook his head. "They didn't talk to me the way Duffy did. He wants to come home with me, Daddy. But Megan has to come with us, too. They've always been together. It wouldn't be right to leave Megan here alone." He looked up at his father with a pleading look that equaled the dog's.

Jack looked to Sandi for help. She smiled and shrugged.

"We really had hoped the two could be adopted together," the attendant said apologetically. "They've been together since they were puppy and kitten."

Jack stared heavenward. "I really don't like cats."

"Megan is litterbox trained, although she enjoys going outside, too," the attendant went on as if he sensed he had a taker. "Duffy's housebroken, very well mannered and gets along with kids and other animals. Both animals were neutered when they were young, so you don't have to worry about anything on that score."

Jack thrust his fingers through his hair. "We don't need any other animals. That dog alone will eat enough for five animals."

"You mean we can have them both!" Patrick hopped up and down. He hugged Sandi then his father. "I'll take really good care of them. You'll see."

"Yeah, you'll learn how to clean up a yard after a dog and clean a litterbox," Jack muttered.

In what seemed like a short time, Jack had paid the adoption fees and was given a leash attached to Duffy's collar, while a yowling Megan was placed in a cardboard pet carrier.

Duffy climbed into the rear seat of the car and sat down as if he was used to being chauffeured around town.

"Daddy, what's neutered?" Patrick asked as Sandi buckled him into his seat.

Jack winced. "Something we don't like to think about."

Sandi shot him a chastising frown. "It means they can't make babies, sweetie."

"Okay." He was satisfied with the simple explanation. Plus, he was too occupied in assuring his new dog and cat they would love their new home. Duffy's reply was a tongue across Patrick's cheek. He giggled.

"No guarantee he'd find a dog, you said," Jack groused, as he started up the engine.

"He kept saying he wanted a puppy. There's no way we could have known a grown-up dog would choose him instead," she explained.

"And a cat," he reminded her.

"Cats are sweet. Very self-sufficient. A law unto themselves."

"Attach themselves to those who hate them most. Shed everywhere. Use their claws on the furniture."

"Shh." She placed her finger against her lips. "Don't give Megan any ideas." When she turned her head, she couldn't help laughing at the scene playing out in the back seat. Duffy had rested his head on the seat back so he was as close to Jack as he could be. As the dog panted, strings of drool hung down from his chin and clung to the fine leather upholstery. "You might want to get a truck for the times you need to transport the animals."

"Can they go to Steffi's wedding?" Patrick asked. "We could give them a bath first."

"I think they'd be happier staying home, Patrick," Sandi told him.

"You do realize that dog is as big as you are," Jack pointed out.

"Yep, but I'm still growing and the man said Duffy is already grown."

"I sure hope he's fully grown, or he'll be eating us out of house and home in no time," Jack muttered.

"We better stop off for dog and cat food," Sandi said, directing him to a nearby chain pet store that carried everything a pet owner could require.

By the time they chose a leash and collars, appropriate toys, food and treats, Jack winced at the total bill.

"Something tells me it won't stop here," he said as he signed the receipt.

"At least they've had their shots," Sandi helpfully offered.

"At least that means we'll only have to worry about getting shots for ourselves." He imagined something crawling up his leg. "And flea collars."

JACK STOOD AT A WINDOW watching Patrick romp with Duffy in the backyard, while Megan explored the house at a leisurely pace. She discovered a window seat in the family room and jumped up onto the padded cover and settled down as if it was made just for her.

Jack smiled as he watched Sandi run out and grab Patrick, spinning him in a circle while Duffy danced around them and barked.

"I love you, Sandi!" Patrick shouted, giving her a smacking kiss.

"And I love my munchkin." She kissed him back.

Just make sure Sandi isn't marrying you for Patrick. Harriet's teasing words passed through his mind.

He wanted anyone who looked after his son to adore Patrick for the wonderful boy he was.

Was it possible Sandi did love Patrick, even wanted him more than Jack?

Jack had never thought of himself as insecure. But right now, insecure was exactly how he felt. A strange sensation settled deep inside him that felt like a raw nagging ache.

Their time alone was rare and precious. Did she look at him the way she looked at Patrick, with love so free and open?

Jack wasn't used to experiencing jealousy. Especially when it had to do with his own son.

"THIS IS BEAUTIFUL." Sandi closed her eyes, threw back her head and breathed in the tangy air. She opened her eyes and picked up her glass of wine.

She and Jack were relaxing on the deck outside the family room after Sandi had put Patrick to bed. Patrick begged for Duffy and Megan to sleep with him, but

Jack explained they would be happier in their own beds. Duffy's bed was in a corner of the laundry room, with Megan's wicker basket nearby. Both adults couldn't miss that Megan preferred the window seat, while Duffy enjoyed sprawling under the kitchen table—his favorite spot during dinner, where, no doubt, he hoped to receive handouts. Sandi put a stop to that after Patrick slipped him a small piece of chicken.

"That dog ate two bowls of kibble this afternoon and didn't slow down until he had two cans of dog food tonight," Jack said, sipping his own drink. He eyed Sandi's legs, which she'd stretched out so she could brace her feet on the deck railing.

Her toenails were painted a deep bronze.

"He and Patrick played pretty hard today." She slowly moved her head from side to side. "Patrick started falling asleep in the tub during his bath. He kept insisting all Duffy would need is a bath and a bow tie for Steffi's wedding, but I explained Duffy would be happier here. The rehearsal is going to be held the evening before the wedding. Patrick is excited about the idea of watching the sunrise. I told him he better make sure he concentrates on the ceremony and not watching the sunrise. He knows it means he'll have to get up very early and has promised to be good about getting up."

"His getting up that early will be a miracle," he said dryly, tracing the outline of his wineglass with his fingers.

"My getting up that early will be a miracle, too," she joked. "I know it will throw Patrick's body clock off, but I don't think one day will hurt him."

"You'd know best."

She turned to look at him, puzzled by the blandness of his tone.

"Would you rather he not participate?"

Jack shook his head. "He's much too excited about the wedding. I guess it's just the craziness of the past few days."

Sandi pushed herself out of her chair and walked over to Jack. She settled herself in his lap and draped her arms around his neck.

"If I didn't know better, I'd think you were suffering from PMS. Want me to break out some chocolate?" She combed her fingers through his hair in a slow caressing sweep. "Or—" she blew softly against the curve of his ear "—me?" she asked in a husky voice.

He was silent for so long, she wondered if he had even heard her.

"Jack?"

"What kind of chocolate?"

She pulled back so she could look at his face. "Do yourself a favor and choose again."

He grinned. "Does that mean you won't share your chocolate?"

"Not on your life!" She hopped off his lap and held out her hands. "Come on, O'Connor, I want the chance to seduce you."

He allowed her to pull him to his feet. "Never let it be said I refused a lady."

Sandi should have realized that it wouldn't take long for Jack to turn the tables and seduce her.

The bedspread lay on the carpet while the sheets were askew on the bed.

She moaned softly as his hands ran over her body

with sensual familiarity. She opened her eyes so she could look at his face…and looked past him.

"Jack." She tapped his bare shoulder.

He continued nuzzling her neck.

"Jack." A note of desperation had entered her voice. This time her taps turned into punches.

He reared back. "What?"

She pointed to her right.

He turned his head and encountered a pair of big brown eyes. Before he could react, a pink tongue appeared and bathed his face.

"Damn it, Duffy!" He rolled away from Sandi, who'd backed up against the headboard and pulled the sheet up over her.

The dog looked at them and uttered a soft *woof.*

"How did he get in?" Sandi demanded in a high-pitched voice.

"I closed the door," Jack told her. He started to get up, then realized he was naked. He muttered curses about dogs as he blindly reached down toward the carpet and finally retrieved his briefs. He tugged them on and climbed off the bed. "Maybe dogs don't mind having an audience, but it's never been my style." He grabbed Duffy's collar and guided him out of the room. He gave the dog a gentle shove and closed the door after him. He stood there with his hands on his hips while staring at the door for several moments. As if making a decision, he snagged a nearby chair and set it against the door.

"He looked as if he was taking notes," he muttered, walking back to the bed.

Sandi's head was downcast and her shoulders were shaking.

"I'm sorry, honey." He sat on the bed, ready to take her in his arms.

She looked up, but instead of seeing tears, he discovered she was laughing.

"Didn't you see how he had one paw on the bed as if he was ready to climb on here with us?" she choked out, holding her stomach. "He's probably out there telling Megan what he saw." She started laughing so hard tears ran down her cheeks.

"I knew that dog would be trouble," he grumbled.

Sandi wiped her eyes with a corner of the sheet. "The mood is gone?"

He heaved a deep sigh. "More like run off the tracks." He trailed the back of his fingers down her cheek. "But there's one good thing about trains." He leaned forward and brushed his lips over the area his fingers just caressed.

"And what is that?" she whispered.

"They always get back on track."

WHEN SANDI CREPT BACK to her room that morning, she paused long enough to check on Patrick. She quietly returned to Jack's room and gestured for him to follow her.

They returned to Patrick's bedroom doorway and looked in to see Duffy peacefully sleeping on the end of the boy's bed. The dog lifted his head, thumped his tail and dropped his head back to the covers again.

"Something tells me that dog is going to take over our lives," Jack whispered before he and Sandi parted company.

"Something tells me he already has."

Chapter Fourteen

"I told her it would happen! All she's done for the past few months is worry about every little imaginary mark on her face and body. A sneeze was the beginning of a cold. A cough the beginning of pneumonia. She was convinced she'd contract some rare disease right before the wedding. Or that an untreatable acne would infect her face. It's a curse, all right. It's *my* curse!" Sandi paced the floor back and forth, waving her arms around in dangerous circles. "And all her fault!"

Jack leaned back so he wouldn't get hit by arms he was considering lethal weapons.

"Why is it your curse?"

She rounded on him with eyes blazing. "Why? *Why?* Because whatever she thinks she's going to get, *I* get! She thinks she's getting the measles. I get them. She's afraid she'll have a zit the night of an important date, and I'm the one with a zit. We won't even talk about what happened the night before an important field trip in high school." She continued pacing. "And now she's done it. She will appear at her wedding tomorrow morning looking radiant and beautiful, and I'll be the ugly sister once again!"

Jack reached out and grabbed Sandi in midstride, bringing her to a stop. He framed her face with his hands and studied her carefully. He was positive her glare was meant to kill him. He racked his brain for the right thing to say.

"It...could be worse."

Sandi stared at him as if he'd lost his mind.

"Just a little extra makeup and no one will even notice," he went on, aware he was digging his grave even deeper. "Maybe some concealer?"

She spat out what he could do with concealer and stalked out of the room.

Jack sighed and collapsed in a chair.

"At least I didn't ask her if PMS had anything to do with it," he muttered. "Then I truly would have been dead."

Memories suddenly swamped his mind. Memories of Michelle throwing a tantrum because she was convinced her hemline didn't hang right. That a lipstick color didn't do her justice. Times when being out of her favorite coffee could send her into a snit for the entire day. A day when he would do whatever was possible to lure her into a loving mood.

How many times had he done just that, until he'd realized what a fool he was and just plain stopped. That was when he realized what a farce their relationship was. He'd told her he had come to his senses and sent the housekeeper in to help her pack.

Five weeks later, she called him to inform him she was pregnant.

It took three years for Jack to realize that Michelle had told him she was pregnant as a bargaining chip. If she hated him as much as she claimed, he knew she would have had an abortion, but she somehow thought she would eventually return to his house, and his bed, as if nothing had happened.

The only good thing that had come from the relationship was Patrick.

"Why can't I wear my tuxedo tonight?" Patrick whined, dragging his feet as he came into the room. He pulled himself up into his father's lap. "Sandi said the rehearsal is like practicin' for the wedding. Can't I practice wearing my tuxedo?"

"Not if we want it clean for the wedding."

"Please?" He hugged his father tightly, giving him his most engaging smile and expression.

"Forget the soulful gaze, kid. You'll wear what Sandi laid out for you to wear. The tuxedo is for tomorrow."

Patrick's lower lip jutted out. Jack playfully pushed it back in.

"You don't want to wear that tuxedo out too soon," he teased.

Patrick nestled closer to his father. "Daddy, when are you going to marry Sandi?"

Jack's heart skipped a beat. Funny how he'd started taking their imaginary engagement for granted. As if it was a sure thing.

"That's up to Sandi."

"But you told Grandma you're going to marry Sandi," he persisted.

"That's still something between Sandi and me," Jack told him.

"I love Sandi a lot and she says she loves me," Patrick said proudly.

Jack hugged him back. "Yes, she does love you a lot," he said quietly. "And that makes you a very lucky boy."

WHEN SANDI LATER EMERGED from her bedroom, Jack couldn't believe she was the same raving woman he'd seen a couple of hours earlier. The beginning of a red rash on her cheek was virtually invisible.

Not that anyone would be looking at her face.

Sandi's short skirt was taupe silk and edged with matching lace. Her camisole-style top was the same color. She'd twisted her hair up, held with a gold clip and left tendrils as wisps against her cheeks. Green eyes looked smoky and mysterious as they gazed at him.

He wasn't surprised to see that her nails were painted a pearly taupe. Her high-heeled sandals were more straps than substance.

She looked downright sexy, and he wanted nothing more than to delve under all that silk.

When he put his arm around her, he noticed she smelled even better.

"Saying that you look gorgeous would be an understatement," he murmured in her ear.

She smiled. "Be careful, O'Connor, or you just might get lucky later on tonight," she murmured back.

"Then I guess I better not behave."

She smoothed a collar that didn't need smoothing and straightened a tie that was already in line.

"You in a suit is downright sinful," she said under her breath. "I think the odds of your getting lucky have just gone up."

Jack grinned. "And I don't even have to fly to Vegas."

SANDI HAD LIKED GREG from the beginning and felt he was a perfect match for her sister.

Six feet tall with blond hair kept in a conservative

cut, he looked as comfortable in his dark blue suit that matched his eyes as he did in casual clothing. And the look of love that fairly radiated from him every time he looked at Steffi was enough to tear into Sandi's heart.

"What happened to your face?" Steffi asked, peering at Sandi's cheek.

She glared at her sister. "What do you think? It's your curse, so it became my curse. I'm going on record now as saying if you have any fears during your pregnancy you are *not* to tell me."

Steffi ignored her order and continued examining Sandi's face. "What concealer did you use? It did an excellent job."

"Keep it up, Steff, and I'll tell Greg about every stunt you've pulled since kindergarten," Sandi chimed. "And I won't leave a thing out. Including," she said in a mock whisper, "what went on in our junior year. You know what I mean. Behind the bleachers during the basketball game with Monterey High in our junior year."

Steffi's nostrils flared. She stared at her between narrowed eyes as she absorbed the threat. "You wouldn't dare."

"Sister, dear, by now you know very well not to dare me."

Steffi looked past Sandi toward Jack. "There was that sorority party our sophomore year in college," she mused.

Sandi threw her arms around her sister and kissed her cheek. "I'll keep your secrets if you'll keep mine," she whispered.

"Deal," she whispered back. "Now you better introduce Jack to Mom and Dad before they think you have something to hide.''

Something to hide? Sandi preferred not to think about that. She kept a smile on her face as she grabbed hold of Jack's arm.

"I don't want to lie to my parents," she said to him between smiling lips.

"Meaning, I shouldn't mention we sleep together." He didn't wince when she pinched his side.

"You know very well what I mean." Her head swiveled from left to right until she found her prey.

Sandi felt butterflies take over her stomach as she led Jack toward her parents.

What was she going to do? Her conscience bothered her a little lying to Harriet Anderson, but lying to her parents was definitely worse.

Their ruse had gone so far, she wondered if they would ever be able to spring loose from it. Not that she wanted to.

The idea of being married to Jack was exhilarating. Teaching her class, coming home to Jack and Patrick. Spending the weekends doing what families do. Maybe a brother or sister for Patrick somewhere along the way.

"Sweetheart, you're squeezing the blood out of my hand," he murmured.

She instantly loosened her grip. "Sorry."

A woman, who looked like an older version of Sandi and Steffi, and the man behind her descended on them.

"Darling!" She threw her arms around Sandi while the man kissed her on the cheek. "You look wonderful." She appraised Jack with a mother's eye.

"That's because she finally got smart and dumped

that idiot Doug," the man muttered. He studied Jack. "You're not a lawyer, are you? I'm Sandi's father, Frank Galloway."

"I only use them for my own amusement. Jack O'Connor." He held out his hand. "The tornado at the back of the chapel is my son, Patrick."

Elaine Galloway turned her head in that direction. "I'd say he's going to be a heartbreaker in ten years."

"Good thing you didn't have a daughter, or you'd be out buying a shotgun," Frank said candidly. "Of course, there will be fathers out there buying a shotgun once their daughters have gotten a look at your son." He looked at Jack sharply. "I bet a lot of fathers did the same when you came sniffing around their daughters."

"Dad!" Sandi squirmed, feeling embarrassment burn all the way through her body. "You didn't act this way with Greg."

"That's because I've known Greg since he was in diapers. I've just met this guy, and I've been hearing that he's been telling people the two of you are getting married." He kept his attention on Jack.

"Frank, this is Steffi's night," Elaine reminded him, tugging on his arm. "I want you to behave yourself."

"I will," he grumbled as his wife started to lead him away. "For now," he added for Jack's benefit.

"I should have known," Sandi groaned softly, turning to hide her face against Jack's shoulder. "Dad is like a Gila monster when he gets a notion in his head. He won't let go."

"It's expected, teach. He's a father." He hugged her briefly. "As good as this feels, I'm afraid we're going to have to break it up. Your sister is gesturing for you to join the party."

She nodded and spun away.

Jack sat near the rear of the chapel. He watched the coordinator make sure everyone was in place, especially the flower girl and the ring bearer. He smiled at Patrick's self-important expression as he held the pink silk pillow that would hold the rings the next day.

He had attended more than a few weddings in his time. Usually those of college classmates and business associates. But he couldn't remember watching the maid of honor as intently as he watched Sandi walk slowly down the aisle in place of the bride. Greg's brother Mark, as best man, was appointed the stand-in groom. A man who turned out to be as good-looking as the groom.

Jack knew he had no reason to feel jealous and was mollified to notice the polite smile Sandi gave the man. But then he did feel a bit jealous, because her heart-stopping smile appeared. For Patrick.

He rapidly tamped down the emotion. He reminded himself he wouldn't have these thoughts if it hadn't been for Harriet's teasing remark. For some reason, he was taking it to heart and it wasn't necessarily a good idea to do that. He returned his attention to Sandi.

Michelle had stung him badly. Left him suspicious of women. Yet he hadn't felt that suspicion about Sandi. She'd been so open and honest from the beginning, he hadn't had an opportunity to feel suspicious.

Now he was wondering if it would be so bad to make that lie the truth.

"SO WHO EXACTLY IS Jack O'Connor?" Elaine Galloway asked her daughter.

Sandi should have known that having her mother practically on her heels as she entered the ladies' room wasn't a coincidence. She sat on one of the chairs before the lighted mirror and opened her tiny silk purse to pull out her lipstick.

"He was Dylan Montgomery's best man. He's a financial consultant, who relocated here from San Francisco, a single father and he's hired me as his son's nanny for the summer." She reeled off the facts. "As far as I know, there's no insanity or hard-core criminals in his family background. But since Mark is a police officer, I guess you could ask him to run a background check."

"No wonder you prefer teaching five-year-olds. You're still on their age level." Elaine applied her lipstick. She paused. "Darling, are you sure you're not on the rebound after Doug? I don't want you falling from the frying pan into the fire."

Sandi chuckled and shook her head at her mother's use of cliché. "Don't worry, Mom. The minute I learned the truth about Doug, I realized I didn't love him the way I should have. If I had truly loved him, I would have killed him for doing that to me. Instead he's living it up with Miss Implants-and-Liposuction, and I know when the time comes she'll take him for everything he's got."

"Now that's the Sandi I know and love." She got up, and on her way out, patted Sandi's shoulder. "What I've seen of Jack I like."

She set her lipstick on the table and blindly reached for her gloss. "Yes, I do, too."

When Sandi returned to the restaurant, she didn't see Jack at the table. She caught Steffi's eye and made a questioning gesture. Steffi smiled and pointed toward the deck that circled the restaurant. Sandi immediately headed for a door that would lead to it. She soon found

Jack standing at the railing overlooking the water. She walked over to him and put her arms around his shoulders, while resting her cheek against his shoulder. He smiled and covered her arm with his hand.

"Patrick is curled up in his chair, sound asleep," she told him. "I guess we should bundle him up for bed."

"He'll hate missing any of the fun."

The silence between the two was as comfortable as a warm quilt. Sandi kept her cheek on Jack's shoulder, content to breathe in the tangy scent of his cologne coupled with the scent that was uniquely his own. By turning her head slightly, she could see the pounding waves crashing against the rocks below. The half-moon above lent scant light to their surroundings, since they weren't near the dining area of the restaurant, where floodlights lit up the sea for the diners.

Now she knew what she'd told her mother was the truth. She'd never felt a portion for Doug what she felt for Jack. Along with the warm flow of emotions, her senses brought troubling thoughts.

"I lose my twin tomorrow," she said softly.

"Marriage won't lessen the connection between you two," he reminded her.

"But it still won't be the same." She sighed heavily. "I'm happy for Steffi. I really am. She and Greg are the perfect couple, but it still feels strange inside me. For so many years, we've had that connection. Now I feel as if it's already not as strong."

Jack turned so he could hold her in his arms. She snuggled against him. Realizing she must be chilly, he took off his suit coat and draped it around her.

"I wouldn't worry, Sandi. Just now she's too busy thinking about tomorrow. So why don't we take Patrick home, tuck him into bed and then I'll fix you a cup of hot cocoa and tuck you into bed.''

A hint of a smile touched her lips. ''You can fix cocoa?''

He looked affronted she'd even ask. ''Can I fix cocoa? I fix great cocoa. You'll see.'' He pulled the coat around her, making sure she slid her arms into the sleeves.

Patrick didn't stir when Jack picked him up. Nor did he stir as they said their goodbyes and left the restaurant. He only mumbled a few words as Sandi put him to bed.

She went to her room to change her clothing, choosing an ankle-length cotton nightgown the color of tangerines. When she walked into the family room, the rich aroma of chocolate teased her nostrils. Jack sat on the couch with two steaming mugs set on the coffee table in front of him. He'd taken off his tie and rolled up his sleeves.

Sandi curled up next to him and accepted the mug he handed her. As she sipped the hot liquid, she experienced a jolt she didn't expect. She arched an eyebrow in surprise.

''My idea of great cocoa means a hint of crème de menthe,'' he explained, picking up his own mug.

''I'd say your idea has merit.'' She sipped some more.

Jack took the mug out of her hand and set it back on the table.

''You need to be up early in the morning and be bright eyed for your sister's wedding. I added just enough crème de menthe to help you sleep.'' He pulled her against his chest.

She smiled and closed her eyes. ''I seem to sleep

better this way." She opened one eye. "Duffy is locked in the laundry room, right?"

"Last I looked."

She yawned, shifting so she could lay her cheek against his chest. "Good. I hate to think what kind of education we're giving him."

"Maybe we can give him to your sister as a wedding gift."

She giggled. "We just won't tell her about his fascination with watching human behavior." She lifted her head to look at him. "Jack?"

"Hmm?"

"If Duffy is locked in the laundry room, what are we doing here?"

She squeaked with surprise when Jack rolled off the couch and picked her up.

"Excellent question. Let's discuss that further, shall we?"

"Oh goody, my favorite kind of discussion."

SANDI COULD FEEL the tears threatening to fall as she listened to her sister recite the wedding vows. She blinked rapidly to hold them back, telling herself it was only so they wouldn't fall onto the pink silk. She'd made sure to use waterproof mascara for just this reason.

Patrick stood up straight, proudly holding the pink silk pillow with the two wedding bands fastened to it by way of darker pink silk ribbons. When Mark started to undo the ribbons and pick up the rings, Patrick looked down at the pillow, then up at him.

I, Stefanie Alice Galloway, take thee, Gregory Matthew Ellison for my lawfully wedded husband.

"Hey! You can't take them! I'm supposed to keep

'em safe!'' Patrick said fiercely. Mark's hands settled on his shoulders, giving him a warning squeeze.

Sandi caught his attention and placed her forefinger against her lips.

"But he's takin' the rings!"

Soft laughter rippled through the guests.

As Steffi and Greg recited their vows, the morning sun broke through the stained-glass windows, sending shafts of color onto the occupants. A golden glow surrounded the bridal couple.

Don't cry, Sandi. Don't cry. She could hear her mother quietly sobbing and even a few sniffs from her father.

Sandi hadn't had much sleep the night before, thanks to Jack. But she didn't mind. Instead she felt wonderfully relaxed, even if she'd been reluctant to leave her bed that morning. Jack finally coaxed her out with a promise of as much coffee as she could drink. Along with a few kisses. What she hadn't expected was that he'd also push her into a cold shower. Her shrieks were ignored, and she was wrapped in her robe and handed a cup of coffee before he escaped the bathroom.

Jack helped Patrick dress and knot his bow tie. Then he drove Sandi over to the chapel, where she dressed and helped Steffi into her gown.

Considering her sister's penchant for semihysterics before any important event, Steffi was remarkably calm this time.

Sandi jokingly told her she was glad videos were being taken of the prewedding activities, since no one would ever believe that Steffi could look so serene. She was further surprised when Steffi did nothing more than smile.

Now she stood there, witness to her sister's marriage. Since Steffi and Greg wanted to start a family as soon as possible, she wouldn't be surprised if she would be an aunt within a year.

No wonder Sandi wanted to cry. Her twin, her best friend and confidante was abandoning her. She tightened her grip on the flowers and kept a smile on her lips, even though it hurt.

After the minister pronounced them man and wife and introduced them to the guests as Mr. and Mrs. Ellison, Greg kissed Steffi.

Then Sandi did cry. She was grateful for Mark's assisting arm as she walked back up the aisle. Through the haze of tears, she saw Jack seated halfway back. She held his smile in her heart as she finished the walk.

"He shouldn't a taken the rings!" Patrick could be heard grumbling. "I'm gettin' really tired of guys taking the rings from *my* pillow."

"You're such a dork. You don't know anything," the flower girl informed him with the worldly air of a seven-year-old.

"Hey, you're the dork. I didn't drop all the flowers on the floor."

JACK STOOD OFF TO THE SIDE, watching the photographer arrange the wedding party for photographs. Sandi got Patrick to smile after explaining to him what a good ring bearer he was and that it was all right for Mark to take the rings since that was his job.

In her off-the-shoulder gown and fingertip veil, Sandi looked like a vision in the early-morning light.

Considering the hour the wedding had been held, the chapel had been packed with guests. He figured it had to do with their wanting to be part of a dawn wedding.

The reception hall at the inn was also filled with guests milling around the tables.

The moment the wedding party finished the first dance, Jack moved in to steal Sandi from Mark.

"Here." He pushed his handkerchief into her hand after he'd smoothed the tears from under her eyes.

"I promised myself I wouldn't cry," she sniffed.

"Easier said than done." He brought her closer to him. "Are you still thinking about a midnight wedding?"

"That was just a joke." She looked at him intently as if she was afraid to breathe.

"Sunset sounds good," he said conversationally. "On the beach." He smiled. "Sweetheart, your mouth is open."

"It's just that you're talking about it as if…as if…"

"As if it's real. Why not?" He twirled her around. "Is there any reason why we shouldn't?"

"I…" She shook her head as if she couldn't believe what she was hearing.

"Funny thing, Sandi. All of a sudden I realized I was in love with you. Something I hadn't expected, I might add," he continued as nonchalantly as if he were talking about the weather. "I'd like the privilege of waking up next to you every morning instead of watching you sneak out of my room or my sneaking out of yours so Patrick won't see us together. You wouldn't mind the idea of Patrick, would you?"

Sandi released her hand from around him long enough to wipe her eyes and blow her nose. "No," she whispered. "I love both of you."

"I hope you might love me in a little different way

than you love him," Jack joked. He suddenly turned serious. His eyes darkened with an emotion that shook her to her core. "Are you willing to go all the way, Sandi? I can promise you that I'll never give you any reason to doubt me."

"This started because of Patrick," she said softly, still sounding unsure.

Jack smiled. "Then he shouldn't object at our taking it to the next level, should he?"

Still wide-eyed, she shook her head.

"You don't mind if I dance with my daughter, do you?" George said, tapping Jack on the shoulder.

Jack smiled and stepped back. "Not at all. In fact, I think I will steal your wife away."

"If you can get her to forget visiting New England during the fall foliage, you can have her."

"Daddy!"

George beamed. "Still my baby."

Sandi looked over her father's shoulder as George guided her across the floor. She blushed a bright red when Jack blew her a kiss.

"If Steffi sees you doing that, she'll be launching her bouquet right at Sandi's face," Elaine teased Jack when she stepped toward him.

"She probably will anyway."

Before Steffi and Greg could even cut the cake, Patrick was using two chairs as a bed.

"I would say the ring bearer has had enough of the wedding reception," Karl told Jack.

Jack smoothed Patrick's hair back from his forehead. The boy didn't stir.

"He'll be pretty mad he missed the party, but considering the hour it began, I guess he did pretty well."

"And when will we attend your wedding, Jack?" Karl asked.

"There were two other weddings to worry about first," he replied. "And a house to settle in."

"And I understand a dog and cat to finish the household." Karl smiled. "Do not wait too long, Jack. Or Patrick will be in college before he has a baby brother or sister." He patted Jack on the back before moving away.

Jack looked back at Patrick, then over at Sandi, who was chattering away to friends.

He was right. Steffi made sure to throw the bouquet straight at Sandi.

He knew immediately that there was no way he could let another man catch the garter.

Chapter Fifteen

"How many mimosas did I have?" Sandi asked as she followed Jack into the house. She carried a plate of wedding cake while he carried Patrick, who was still asleep.

"Enough to be the mournful twin when Steffi and Greg left on their honeymoon."

She groaned. "I can't believe I was as bad as Mom. No one else needed to cry. We did enough for everyone there."

"True." He carried Patrick to his room, quickly divested him of his now wrinkled tuxedo and tucked him into bed. "Down, Duffy," he ordered the dog who lay at the end of the bed.

Duffy lifted his head, whined and dropped it back down on his paws again.

"Note to myself. Check into obedience schools," he muttered, leaving the room.

When he reached the family room, Sandi was stretched out on the couch with Megan sprawled on her stomach. The cat seemed to understand not to dig her claws into the silk fabric. Sandi absently stroked the cat's back while the feline purred her contentment.

"A dog who doesn't behave. A cat who leaves a ton of fur everywhere she lands," he complained.

"Petting an animal lowers your blood pressure and stress levels," she informed him.

"Gives you fleas."

"The flea dip took care of that problem, and Duffy's on flea medication now. Megan is too arrogant to have fleas." She fingered the rhinestone collar that circled the cat's neck. The tiny bell attached to it tinkled a merry song in reply. Sandi had added the bell after the first time Megan left a mangled bird on the kitchen steps. Jack dispensed with it before Patrick could see it.

Jack pushed aside the items on the coffee table and sat down facing Sandi.

"So what do you think, teach? Can we make it together?"

Her lips tipped upward. "Gee, I thought we already had," she intoned. "More than once."

Jack muttered a curse. "Sandi."

She picked up on his warning. "Sorry. I guess the mimosas were more than I needed this morning. It was all those toasts that did me in." She picked up Megan and set her to one side. The cat meowed her displeasure and jumped off the couch. She headed for her window seat and curled up on the cushion.

"I think I was subconsciously heading this way when I went along with Patrick's story and when I gave you full rein to decorate the house," Jack said. "Even then I knew I wanted your influence in every room."

Sandi rolled over onto her side, bracing her head on her palm.

"I'm not in your social class, Jack. My idea of great

art is an orange elephant done with fingerpaints. To me, good wine is any wine that tastes good and I worked my way through school. I was a waitress at a pizza place and couldn't eat the stuff for three years after I left there. Mrs. Montgomery was right. I'm not nanny material. I'm a kindergarten teacher, who just happens to be good at her job. If you really want the right kind of wife, have Mrs. Montgomery or Mrs. Anderson find one for you.''

"I want a wife who understands what family means. Someone who will love my kid. And love me. That's what matters.'' He took her hand and brought her fingers to his lips. "Sandi, when I make love to you, I feel as if I've come home.''

She blinked rapidly. "Damn you, O'Connor. You're going to make me cry again.''

Jack nibbled on her fingers. "Don't cry at our wedding, all right? People might think I'm forcing you into it.'' His gaze was somber as he regarded her. "We're good together, Sandi. Patrick adores you. I adore you and love you. Anything more you want to know?''

She kept sniffing. "Keep going.''

"You're the only one who can make the dog behave and the only one that damned cat seems to like.''

"So you want me for my pet maintenance skills.'' Her smile was watery.

Jack proceeded to tell Sandi exactly what he wanted her for in very explicit terms.

"I'm positive that what you're talking about is illegal in several states,'' she told him, desire burning in her gaze. "Not to mention there's a five-year-old child in the house who might wake up at anytime.''

Jack stood up and bent down, pulling Sandi into his arms. He headed for his bedroom.

"Then I guess we should be very quiet."

He didn't set her down on her feet until he stood by his bed. He turned her around, efficiently lowered the zipper and slipped the dress down her arms and to her waist. He murmured his appreciation for the blush-colored strapless bra and bikini panties, complete with matching thigh-high stockings.

"Your attire gives me some interesting ideas." He took the pins out of her hair, combing it free with his fingers.

"Are we talking illegal in certain states again?" She did her part by loosening his bow tie and pulling it from his collar. She began releasing his shirt studs next. The tangy smell of starched cotton mixed with his own scent teased her nostrils. The soft cotton of his T-shirt tantalized her fingertips as she smoothed her palms across the hard contours of his chest. She tilted her head to one side and nibbled kisses along the side of his neck as she slid the belt free and un-zipped his slacks. She kept up the string of kisses as she pushed his slacks downward.

"I won't give up my teaching," she murmured, nipping the skin along his collarbone.

"I wouldn't expect you to." He captured her silk-covered nipples with his thumbs and gently rubbed in a circular motion. He smiled his satisfaction as the tips peaked from his touch. Except he wanted more. He dipped his head and covered the silk with his mouth.

Sandi gripped his shoulders as he first dampened the fabric with his mouth then blew on it.

"Jack," she whimpered, digging her fingertips into his skin as she held on for dear life.

"Do you know how incredibly sexy you look?" he murmured, tracing the delicate bones across her shoulders and down to the top of her breasts that plumped out over the lacy top of the bra. His touch blazed a trail down to her navel and along the narrow strip of panties. He smoothed along her hipbone and down to her thigh. He pushed aside one leg to find her moist core. She whimpered his name as he inserted his finger, then two.

"You don't play fair," she moaned, slightly moving her legs apart to give him better access.

"You never did. You blew into my life like a breath of fresh air, and I still haven't recovered." Even as his fingers began a distinct rhythm, his mouth covered hers in a drowning kiss.

Sandi had no idea how she ended up lying on the bed. Or how Jack wound up beside her. Then inside her.

As she looked up into his face, she saw an intensity that took her breath away. And a love that stole her heart. When she felt her own body begin to quicken, she lifted her head and touched her lips to his. As she felt his body tighten and begin to thrust faster, she felt him cry her name into her mouth even as she cried his. And they shot up into the stars together.

"And Steffi thought Tahiti would be the ultimate," Sandi said drowsily as she curled up in Jack's arms and promptly fell asleep.

Jack leaned back against his pillow and closed his eyes. "Always nice to be thought the ultimate."

WHEN JACK OPENED HIS EYES, he realized he'd slept a little over an hour. He crept out of bed quietly, not wanting to disturb Sandi, who still slept deeply. Yawning, he walked into the bathroom and turned on the shower.

When he stepped into the stall, he looked at the shower caddy set in one corner of the large unit. Along with his shampoo and soap were containers holding Sandi's shampoo and conditioner and a tube of one of her favorite scented shower gels. He picked up the tube and squeezed out a small dollop. He rubbed it between his fingers and brought it to his nose. Lemon-lime. He was never sure what he'd find in here.

Jack hummed softly as he ducked his head under the spray then applied shampoo. He was rinsing his hair when he felt the shower door click then a brief draft of cool air.

"Woke up, did you?" He turned around, but found nothing other than the shower door ajar.

A sound had him looking down. He backed up so suddenly, he almost slipped on the floor.

"Damn it all to hell!"

Sandi shot upright at the sound of Jack's shout. She bolted out of bed and ran to the bathroom, all the while fearing the worst.

"What's wrong?" she gasped. She stared at the open shower door. "Jack? Answer me!"

"Damn it, look!"

She looked into the cubicle to find him braced against a corner. He pointed downward.

"I can't believe I'm seeing this," she said, unsure whether to laugh or take him seriously.

Megan stood under the warm spray, unconcerned that she was getting wet. If anything, she looked as if she was enjoying her shower.

"Cats hate water," Jack snarled. "We get one that

loves it. Dogs shouldn't be able to open doors, but we get one that can. What next?''

"A hamster that sings opera? Sorry." Her apology for her tongue-in-cheek quip didn't come off completely sincere. She grabbed a towel and reached in for the cat. "Honestly, Megan, if you wanted a bath you only had to say so," she murmured to the cat as she wrapped her in the towel and began drying her. She plugged in the hair dryer and set the cat on the counter. She began sweeping warm air over the cat, combing her fur with her fingers to help speed up the drying process.

"I refuse to share my shower with a cat," he stated emphatically, reaching for a towel and wrapping it around his hips.

"I'm surprised she hasn't done it before," Sandi mused, continuing to dry the cat's heavy fur. She grabbed a comb and began smoothing the fur.

Jack just stared at her. She looked at him as if to say, "What?"

"My comb."

She grimaced. "Sorry again. I didn't want her fur to get all tangled."

The cat purred her happiness at the attention paid to her. She curved a paw around Sandi's wrist.

"You are one spoiled cat, do you know that?" she cooed.

"Spoiled is an understatement," Jack groused, using his fingers to comb his wet hair back from his face.

"Next time you want a shower, Megan, come in with me," Sandi said as she picked her up and set her on the floor. The cat sauntered out of the room with her plume of a tail curved over her back. Sandi looked over at Jack. "Okay, handsome. Your turn." She directed him to the stool in front of the mirror and had him sit down. She stood behind him with the hair dryer and another comb, drying his hair. When she was satisfied with her job, she turned off the dryer.

"Half-naked woman styling man's hair. I like this idea," Jack commented.

It wasn't until his remark that she thought to look in the mirror.

Sandi's bra had disappeared sometime during their lovemaking, but she still wore her thigh-high stockings, which now looked the worse for wear. Her hair was tangled and her makeup smudged.

"I won't even say what I look like." She headed for the shower and turned on the water. "And don't even think it!" she warned as she peeled off the stockings and tossed them in the wastebasket. She stepped into the cubicle and shut the door.

"Personally I thought you looked pretty hot," he raised his voice to be heard. "How about I wake up the munchkin and we go out to lunch?"

"How about you wake up the munchkin and I fix a picnic lunch we can take to the beach?"

"Let's compromise. I'll wake up the munchkin and we'll pick up a lunch at the deli to take to the beach."

"Fine." Her voice was muffled under the shower spray.

When Jack went into Patrick's room, he found his son under the covers with Duffy stretched out beside him, his head sharing the pillow.

"Do you have any idea how much that fancy dog bed cost?" he muttered to the dog. He gently shook Patrick's shoulder and said his name.

Patrick slowly opened his eyes and looked up at his father. At first, he looked confused then realization hit.

"I missed everything!" he wailed.

"Don't worry, Sandi brought home some cake for you," Jack assured him. "You just needed a nap, that's all. But you did great at the wedding ceremony. And to celebrate, we thought we'd go to the beach and take a picnic lunch."

His eyes lit up. "Can Duffy go with us?"

The dog lifted his head as he heard his name.

"If he goes, he has to stay on the leash. That's the law."

"But he can go with us and run even if he's on the leash, right?" the boy asked hopefully.

Jack nodded, aware he was going to lose the battle, no matter what.

"But the cat stays home." That battle he'd win, no matter what.

"Megan wouldn't like the beach anyway. Cats don't like water." Patrick climbed out of bed and ran to his chest of drawers.

"That's what you think," Jack muttered, staying to make sure his son chose clothing that matched or at least didn't clash too horribly.

"SUMMER'S ALREADY COMING to an end," Sandi said, lifting her face to the sun. "I can feel the shift in the air."

"You really were a beach babe, weren't you?" Jack teased.

She nodded. "When we reached high school, Steffi and I worked at the beach every summer in one of the food shacks. The pay was lousy, but the view was spectacular."

"Not to mention all the boys."

"That, too." She pulled her knees up and wrapped her arms around them. "Look at them."

Jack followed her gaze and watched Patrick holding on to the leash for dear life as he raced up and down the beach. The dog, as if sensing his young master's legs couldn't keep up with him, kept his stride shorter than usual.

"He's going to be in seventh heaven when we tell him about us," Jack said, moving until he sat behind her. He spread his legs and pulled her back against his chest. When she leaned back, he draped his arms around her.

She relished the warmth of his body and the security of his embrace. She curved one arm behind her and around his neck so she could bring his face to hers for a kiss.

"Hey! Whatcha doing that for?" Patrick ran up and dropped to his knees. Duffy lay down panting. Patrick screwed up his face with distaste.

"You'll understand when you get older," Jack told him.

"Come kiss me, my frog, and I will turn you into a handsome prince." Sandi opened her arms wide to Patrick.

He leaned over and gave her a smacking kiss on the cheek.

"*Ribbit!*" He grinned, looking like a younger version of his father.

"I guess we'll have to dig a pond in the backyard for you, frog." Sandi ruffled his hair.

"How come you two kiss so much?" he asked, picking up a carrot stick and munching on it.

"Because I like kissing Sandi and she likes kissing

me," Jack explained. "What do you think, Patrick, should we keep Sandi?"

"We got her now."

"I mean for always. Maybe I should marry Sandi."

His eyes widened. "For real?"

Jack nodded. "For real. For always."

Patrick turned to Sandi for confirmation. She smiled and nodded.

"Cool!" He threw his arms around her and kissed her again. Then he jumped up and did a dance around them.

"I guess that means he's all for the idea," Jack said dryly.

Sandi chuckled. "Yes, I guess so."

"Then I do believe we should seal the deal." He grasped her chin with his fingertips and brought her face to his for a kiss.

"Yuck!" Patrick shouted when he saw them.

But they didn't hear him. They were too involved in sealing the deal.

Chapter Sixteen

"I can't do this." Sandi hung back and dug in her heels.

Jack, who'd been holding her hand, easily felt her resistance. He halted and looked back. His frown was pure confusion at the look on her face.

"What do you mean you can't do this? It's part of the ritual. When two people get engaged, the man buys the woman an engagement ring. That's what we're doing," he reminded her. "You didn't act leery about it this morning when I said I wanted to get you a ring."

"I guess I didn't realize we were coming here to get it," she murmured.

Sandi looked at the store windows, displaying elegant jewelry. She could remember passing the store on numerous occasions but never entering. It was just too intimidating. The stuff in there was definitely very real and very expensive.

She'd seen people wearing items bought here, but she didn't think there was anything in there she would be seen wearing without a security alarm attached to it.

She didn't want a diamond ring that came with its

own bodyguard. She didn't want potential thieves scoping out her ring.

Jack stepped forward and rested his hands on her shoulders, gently rubbing his thumbs along the side of her neck.

"This ritual is pretty much painless, teach. Some women even think it's fun," he teased. "I promise, it'll be painless. Come in here with me, and after we're finished, we'll do something you want to do. How does that sound?"

She looked suspicious. "It sounds like a bribe."

He smiled. "Whatever works." He kissed her on the forehead, then rested his forehead against hers. "Come on, Sandi. Let's find the perfect ring for you."

Sandi took several deep breaths and forced herself to relax. By the time they stepped inside the store, she felt more like herself. Muted strains of Mozart could be heard in the background. She reminded herself she'd been inside jewelry stores before. She and Steffi had gotten their mother a sapphire pendant once. "We'd like to look at some engagement rings," Jack explained.

"Of course." The man beamed as he led them to a glass table with two velvet-covered chairs. He gestured for them to be seated.

"I feel as if I'm living my own version of *Pretty Woman*," Sandi leaned over and whispered to Jack when the manager moved over to the case to select some rings.

"Except I'm better looking than Richard Gere," he whispered back.

"I'll get back to you on that." She barely squelched a yelp when he pinched her on the bottom. She recovered in time to give the manager a brilliant smile.

He looked uncertain for a moment, then returned a paler imitation of his own.

Sandi inwardly cringed when she looked at the rings the man displayed on a square of black velvet. There was no mistake that all were beautiful. All were uniquely designed. And all were much more than she cared to have.

Jack frowned as he inspected each one. "They are lovely, but I don't feel they're what we're looking for."

The manager paled, fearing he would lose a lucrative commission. "I'm afraid we don't have any larger stones just now, but I can look for anything you wish. Perhaps you'd even consider a custom design."

"Definitely not a larger stone. These are too large as it is," Jack said. "The lady has delicate fingers and requires a delicate ring. They'd only weigh her hand down. I'd like to find something that would suit her."

The manager murmured, "May I?" and picked up Sandi's left hand. After examining it, he went into the back of the store.

In a few moments, he returned carrying a black velvet box. He placed it on the table and carefully opened it.

"Perhaps this will suit the lady."

Sandi took one look and fell in love. It took all of her willpower not to reach out and snatch up the ring and insist it was hers.

The platinum band was plain, except for faint etching on each side of the diamond, which seemed to give off blue flashes of light.

"A perfect two carat blue diamond," the manager proudly declared.

Jack picked it up and examined the ring. He turned

to Sandi and held up her left hand, sliding it onto her ring finger.

She didn't breathe until she realized it was a perfect fit. It could have been made just for her. She lifted her head and gazed at Jack. There were stars in her eyes and a broad smile on her lips. Jack was sorely tempted to kiss her. Except he knew he wouldn't be able to stop with just one.

"I won't give it back," she whispered.

He smiled. "You don't have to." He turned to the manager. "I'd like a pendant and earrings to complement the ring."

The manager's eyes lit up. "Of course, sir. I will take care of it personally."

"And we'd also like to look at wedding bands." He glanced momentarily at Sandi. "Easier than you putting a brand on me. And less painful."

"We need three rings," she said suddenly.

Jack cocked an eyebrow. "Three? Sandra, my love, is there something you haven't told me?"

She ignored his use of her full name. "The third ring is for Patrick. A family ring."

He didn't resist now. He cupped her face with his hands and kissed her as if there was no tomorrow.

"Remind me to continue this later on," he whispered as he drew back.

She looked dazed for a moment but quickly recovered. "No problem there."

The manager, clearly not used to open displays of affection, took a moment before remembering Sandi's request.

A half hour later, they left with the diamond ring still on Sandi's finger and three bands in velvet-covered boxes nestled in a bag Jack carried.

"After people learn Patrick gets a ring, too, they're going to think you're marrying me for him," he joked, sliding his arm around her waist as they walked down the sidewalk.

She slipped her arm around his waist, tucking her hand into his back pocket. She was giddy with delight that she could show people he was all hers.

"What can I say? Guilty as charged. Patrick's a wonderful bonus I couldn't resist latching onto," she said airily. "I've always felt there's nothing better than a package deal, and the two of you are a package I wasn't willing to give up." When she glanced up at him she would have sworn there was a strange look on his face, but it disappeared as quickly as it appeared. She passed it off as her imagination and guided him toward a corner restaurant.

"All that shopping has made me hungry," she informed him. "The least you can do is feed me." She eyed the bakery cases filled with all sorts of desserts and pastries as if she was ready to choose one of each.

Jack noticed the direction of her hungry gaze. "Yes, I can see what you're hungry for. I guess I better feed you fast before you decide to eat the menu."

Once they were seated and had given their order to the waitress, Jack turned to Sandi. He covered her hand with his and laced his fingers through hers. They sat quietly for a bit, admiring her ring and languishing in their happiness.

"Patrick asked me if he'll still be able to have you for a teacher," he told her, after their waitress had deposited their drinks and appetizers. "I told him I didn't think the school would allow it."

"They usually don't," she agreed.

"He's not too happy about that. He said he knows he'd do better if you were his teacher."

Sandi laughed. "He just thinks that because he thinks I'd give him a better grade. He'll do fine. He's a smart kid and quick to catch on."

"So when do you want to have the wedding?"

"Let's not do anything elaborate," she said hastily.

"Sunset on the beach just past the inn," Jack suggested. "Us and our closest friends, so you won't even have to address invitations unless you want to. Maybe Steffi would want to cater the reception."

Her face lit up as she realized what he was suggesting. "Patrick will want to wear his tuxedo." She picked up her glass of iced tea and sipped.

"He might as well, because I think he's starting to outgrow it." Jack picked up one of the cheese-and-bacon-laden potato skins and bit into it.

Sandi selected deep-fried zucchini from the appetizer tray and nibbled. Her expression grew dreamy as she visualized the scene.

"At least Patrick would only require an afternoon nap to stay awake for the party," she said, still smiling. "That will make him happy."

"I think he's been happy since the day I hired you," he said, trying a Buffalo wing next.

She looked down at her ring. "We're so different."

"That's what makes it interesting. I never know what you'll do next," he told her. "And if your sister wants to throw you a party, no Sean."

She affected a pout. "No Sean? But he was the best part of the whole party."

"That's why no Sean."

"That goes both ways. But before we even think

about that, we need to set a date." She racked her brain.

"I don't intend to wait too long," he warned her.

"That's fine with me. And I'd like to have it before Patrick starts school."

"As I said before, I could wonder if you're marrying me for me or for Patrick." Jack smiled at the waitress as she set his salad in front of him.

"If I didn't know any better I'd think you were jealous," she teased, digging into her large spinach salad with hot bacon dressing. "As if you have any reason for it."

Jack didn't want to think that was truly his problem. Yet why did that thought keep cropping up in his mind when, as she said, there was no reason for it?

After lunch, Sandi wanted to browse through a few stores, so Jack stopped in Karl's shop.

"The rumors are circulating that you bought Sandi an exquisite diamond engagement ring. Has a date been set yet?" Karl was busy arranging a dinner jacket on a mannequin.

"Considering we only bought the rings a couple of hours ago, I'd have to say the grapevine is very efficient. As for a date, we're working on it now." He sat down in a chair and stretched out his legs.

"You are a very lucky man, Jack. It is obvious how much Sandi loves Patrick. Often a stepmother isn't that loving toward a stepchild."

"Yes, well, perhaps she wants Patrick more than me," he mused, not even thinking as he spoke.

Karl turned away from the display and walked over to Jack, taking the chair next to him.

"Why can't you believe she truly loves you?" he asked.

Jack rubbed his chin as he thought about it. "Because too many women have told me they wanted me, but what they've really wanted is my money. Hell, I'm sure when I tell J.T., his first question will be whether or not I'm having her sign a prenuptial agreement. After Patrick was born, I was even more careful with relationships, because I didn't want him to become attached to a woman who wouldn't be in his life on a full-time basis."

"Yet you obviously became attached to Sandi," Karl pointed out with a hint of a smile.

Jack stared at the older man. He wondered what Karl knew that he didn't. "She's special."

"Exactly. Which is why you are in love with her. Just as she is in love with you. All a person has to do is look at her and they see her gazing at you with all of her emotions showing. She does not care who knows how she feels about you. That kind of love is very exclusive where two people share what is in their hearts. Sandi may love Patrick, but remember, that is a love a mother has for a child. Her love for you is much deeper. As long as you remember that, and cherish her, you will never be unhappy and you will never be alone."

Jack stared off into the distance, lost in his own thoughts and thinking over what Karl said.

Deep down, he didn't doubt Sandi's love for him. Not given to low self-esteem, it wasn't easy to doubt anyone. Maybe it was due to the upheaval of the move, seeing one of his closest friends succumb to love and the realization that they were all moving on.

He looked at Karl. "Were you ever in love, Karl?"

The man smiled, but there was sorrow in it.

"Love can be glorious and love can be painful.

Alas, mine has been painful, but I hope the time will come when it will be glorious. After all, I am not dead yet," he added on a joking note.

Jack laughed as expected.

"I hope I become as wise as you when I'm your age, Karl." He stood up.

"You will, as long as you cherish your woman."

Jack smiled again and waved as he left the shop with a considerably lighter heart than when he'd entered.

He didn't waste any time in driving home. He knew Patrick was on a play date and wouldn't be back until early evening, so he would have much needed time alone with Sandi.

He called out her name when he entered the house and soon found her seated cross-legged in the middle of her bed. A bottle of lotion sat on the bedside table. She was rubbing her hands and the light scent of orange and vanilla was in the air.

Jack pulled off his shoes and sat on the bed so he could face her.

"A part of me was afraid you loved Patrick more than me and that you were marrying me for him," he confessed.

Her expression grew soft instead of astonished. She reached out and grasped his hands.

"Do you still feel that way?"

He shook his head.

"I didn't come back to Montgomery Beach with the idea of falling in love," she said candidly. "I came back because it was home. Because I feel safe here. I felt it was the perfect place to allow me to nurse my wounds." She rested her palms against his and laced her fingers through his. "Instead, this charming young man informs me I'm not a very good waitress, and he persuades his father to hire me as his nanny. I think your son was playing matchmaker. And I'm glad he did.''

Jack kept hold of her hands as he stretched out on the bed, urging her to do the same. They lay facing each other.

''What do you think? A little sister or a little brother for Patrick?'' Sandi asked in a soft voice.

''You want kids?''

''Don't act so surprised. Of course, I do. As long as they have my looks and your intelligence,'' she said loftily.

He brushed back a stray lock of hair that had drifted onto her cheek.

''I'm sorry I doubted you.''

''If we're confessing, I should tell you I had a few frightening thoughts that I couldn't fit in with the life-style you're so used to,'' she admitted. ''All you had to do was move here and you had an automatic social standing I could only dream about. I don't play golf.''

''It's not one of my favorite games. Probably because I play pretty badly. Tennis is more my game.''

''I can't imagine spending an afternoon playing bridge or planning the next spring dance.''

''Good, because you'll be pretty busy teaching all those future hoodlums,'' he teased. ''I'm not marrying you because I want a trophy wife whose life revolves around social functions. I want a wife who's willing to put up with a husband who might have to get up in the middle of the night to make a call to Hong Kong or Japan. Who tells good bedtime stories, smells nice and will bake cookies for her husband and son.''

She laughed joyously and rolled into him. "That I will do," she said just before she kissed him.

A kiss wasn't enough and soon their clothes lay scattered around the bed. Jack looked into Sandi's eyes as he entered her. The smile on her face was all he needed to know their love was more than enough.

SANDI HAD PLANNED a quiet picnic lunch in Jack's office while Patrick played at a neighbor's house. Since they'd moved here, Patrick had discovered quite a few children his age in the area and Sandi teased him he was becoming quite the popular kid. She was more than willing to trade play dates with mothers.

And afternoons Patrick was gone, she enjoyed time alone with Jack. She shifted the basket from one hand to the other and started to open the door when she heard her name filtering through the partially open window.

"And Patrick was the one to see it first," she could hear Jack say.

She remained quiet by the window, intent on learning who he was talking to.

"What I need is for you to be one of my best men."

She had to assume he was talking to J.T. Watson, since he'd talked to Dylan several days ago.

"I met Sandi here, fell in love here, and Sandi and Patrick and myself are going to make our life here. That's why it's going to start here."

Sandi smiled. The man was so sweet that she'd have to give him an extra big kiss for that. Who was it that had said eavesdroppers never heard good of themselves?

She strained to hear his words; he must have swiveled his chair away from the window, because she could only catch bits and pieces.

"Why are you hedging all over the place, and why don't you want to come here? Let's put it this way, Dylan's the only Montgomery coming to the wedding."

She pulled out a carrot stick and started munching on it. Now what did that mean?

"She won't be here, J.T."

She? The only Montgomery? He can only be talking about Candice. Candice and J.T.? What was that about? Inquisitive minds want to know. She pulled out another carrot stick and bit down.

"You're still mad about what happened.... Just come to my wedding. I need you here."

Sandi remained by the door as Jack finished the call. Even then she counted to twenty-five before she knocked and opened it.

"How about some lunch?" she announced, holding up the picnic basket.

Jack swiveled around in his chair. He looked at the clock on his desk and noted it was just past one. He grinned.

"When does Patrick get back?"

"Not until five." She gave him an arched look as if she knew what was on his mind.

"That should be enough time."

"Enough time for what?" she asked coyly.

"To practice for our honeymoon. I like to know I'll get it right."

Epilogue

A more perfect sunset couldn't have been planned for the wedding. A soft warm breeze blew in and the waves crashed gently on the shore. The setting sun sent a loving red-orange glow over the wedding party and left the participants feeling as if they'd been bathed in golden light.

The bride wore a cream-colored off-the-shoulder gown with billowing lace sleeves. Her hair was pulled up into curls with baby's breath threaded through the curls. The curved neckline of her gown displayed a gold chain with three pearls evenly spaced along the chain. She wore a bracelet with three more pearls, pearl stud earrings and a gold ankle bracelet. Her smile was brilliant and filled with love as she looked at the groom. There was, however, one incongruency.

This bride was barefoot.

As were the formally garbed groom and his best man.

"Three pearls to stand for the three of us," Jack had told Sandi when he'd presented her with his wedding present the night before. "We'll talk about additional pearls later on when the babies come."

She'd predictably cried and hugged him tightly.

"I now pronounce you man and wife," the minister intoned. "You may kiss the bride."

"The best part," Jack whispered as he kissed Sandi a lot more thoroughly than expected at a wedding. He didn't draw back until Dylan and J.T. insisted on their turn. And Patrick demanded a kiss of his own.

"Ladies and gentlemen, I would like to present to you Mr. and Mrs. Jack O'Connor," the minister announced.

Jack picked Sandi up in his arms and spun her around in a circle. She laughed and threw her arms out to embrace the world she felt was hers. Patrick laughed shrilly and danced around them.

"I got a mom!" he announced. "I got a mom!"

"And this is for my beach baby," he said, still carrying her and walking into the water.

"Jack!" She threw her arms around his neck to keep her balance.

He ignored her entreaty as he waded out until he was knee-deep in the water. He looked at her and smiled.

Sandi didn't guess his intent until it was too late. She screamed just as he opened his arms and she fell into the water. But she had the presence of mind to reach out and push him off balance so that he also fell into the water.

"Neat!" Patrick shouted, hopping up and down on the beach.

"Like I said, a package deal," Sandi told Jack, her arms back around his neck. "What happens to you, happens to me."

"Definitely no boredom here." He kissed her. "No wonder I love you."

Karl stood on the beach watching the couple kiss and laugh. There was no doubt they would have a good life together.

He smiled. He only hoped his luck would hold.

Looking For More Romance?

Visit Romance.net

Check in daily for these and other exciting features:

Hot off the press

View all current titles, and purchase them on-line.

What do the stars have in store for you?

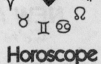

Horoscope

Hot deals

Exclusive offers available only at Romance.net

Plus, don't miss our interactive quizzes, contests and bonus gifts.

PWEB

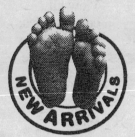

At Karl Delaney's tux shop you get more than a bow tie and cummerbund, you get free advice on your love life. As Karl says, "You don't own a tux shop for forty years and not know a little something about romance."

Join friends Dylan, Jack and J.T. as they pick up their tuxes and find surprise messages in their pockets.

SUDDENLY A DADDY
Mindy Neff April 1999

THE LAST TWO BACHELORS
Linda Randall Wisdom May 1999

COWBOY IN A TUX
Mary Anne Wilson June 1999

DELANEY'S GROOMS—Tuxedo rentals and sales—matchmaking included!

Available at your favorite retail outlet.

Makes any time special ™

COMING NEXT MONTH

#777 SURPRISE—YOU'RE A DADDY! by Judy Christenberry
4 Tots for 4 Texans
Spence Hauk never forgot that night when he made love to Melanie Rule.
She was everything he'd wanted, even though she was in love with another
man. But now that Melanie is carrying his child, the rugged cowboy wants
his family—baby *and* wife.

#778 COWBOY IN A TUX by Mary Anne Wilson
Delaney's Grooms
Cowboy J. T. Watson disliked weddings—some years ago he'd been the
groom in one that lasted one night. But this cowboy's on a run of bad
luck when his ex, Candice, ends up his partner at his friend's nuptials...
and he finds a message in his tux that says, "You're still married!"

#779 DIAMOND DADDIES by Linda Cajio
Every man's greatest fortune is his family. Only, twin brothers and
confirmed bachelors Jeff and Julian Diamond don't know it yet. So their
matchmaking grandfather is determined to make sure they have incentive
to marry and give him grandbabies—plus a hefty tax break—by the end
of the year.

#780 STUD FOR HIRE? by Debbi Rawlins
When a stranger tried to hire Adam Knight to romance her "poor,
heartbroken" friend, Adam said "No way!" But the next thing he knew,
"poor" Gracie Allen had stolen his heart. Would she ever believe it when
she learned his secret?

Look us up on-line at: http://www.romance.net